'I thought you might still be nettled by our encounter last night.'

Alison opened her eyes wide in mock surprise. 'Really? I don't know why. You only yelled at me, bullied me and manhandled me. Why should I be annoyed?'

'I had my reasons.' It was a curt statement, making it clear that, whatever his reasons were, he wasn't going to explain them.

'I'm glad to hear it,' Alison conceded drily. 'I'd hate to think you behaved like that for fun.'

This time he laughed out loud, his eyes flicking over her with shrewd interest. 'For fun . . . I haven't heard that expression in a long time. No, Miss Taylor, that's certainly not what I do for fun.'

Licking her lips in an unconsciously provocative gesture, she observed gravely, 'How very reassuring.'

His eyes held hers. 'Do you need reassurance?' he asked softly, sexily, making the perfectly innocuous word sound positively debauched.

WELCOME THE SUNRISE

BY

LIZA HADLEY

MILLS & BOON LIMITED
ETON HOUSE   18-24 PARADISE ROAD
RICHMOND   SURREY   TW9 1SR

First published in Great Britain 1989
by Mills & Boon Limited

© Liza Hadley 1989

Australian copyright 1989
Philippine copyright 1989
This edition 1989

ISBN 0 263 76247 5

Set in Palacio 10 on 11½ pt.
01 – 8903 – 58175

Typeset in Great Britain by JCL Graphics, Bristol

Made and printed in Great Britain

CHAPTER ONE

WITH quick, deft movements, Alison towelled herself
dry and pulled on clean jeans and a warm, baggy
sweatshirt; it was still only May, and the temperature
dropped sharply in the evenings, making some
winter clothing essential. A quick comb through was
all it took to sweep the damp tendrils of auburn hair
back off her face, plastering its short length to her
scalp. She could dry it off properly back at the tent.
Then, gathering up her towel and soap-bag and
briefly checking to see she hadn't left anything
behind, she slid back the bolt on the cubicle door.

The shower had been an unaccustomed luxury and
she'd spent longer then intended in there, so that
now, emerging from the pine cabin-style building,
Alison discovered that the dusk of twilight had been
replaced by a penetrating darkness. She paused
uncertainly; this shower block was situated in the
wooded area of the camp-site, farthest from the main
complex and not a section she was yet familiar with.
An eerie, disorientating silence had descended with
the darkness, punctuated only by the occasional
rustlings and hootings of small animals and birds—at
least, she hoped it was just the wildlife! A few
seconds' pause allowed her eyes to adjust to the pitch
blackness and ascertain her bearings sufficiently to
locate the path leading back to the centre.

She had already progressed a few yards along it when, without warning, a bat swooped out of the trees, so low it seemed as if it must hit her, but in fact just skimming over her head. She was more startled than frightened, but a piercing scream nevertheless escaped her before she could suppress it. It was an involuntary reaction, and as soon as the sound died on her lips her cheeks flushed with embarrassed warmth. 'Idiot', she reproached herself out loud, thankful there hadn't been anyone else about to hear her foolishness. But at that moment crunching footsteps sounded on the gravelled path and the tall figure of a man detached itself from the shadows and loomed into profile. Alison put her hands up to her lips to stifile a second scream, just as the man's voice rang out to harshly bridge the distance between them. 'Be quiet, you little fool.'

The accent was unmistakably French, the tone unmistakably angry. In an instant, annoyance replaced anxiety and Alison felt the previous blush of embarrassment flame into irritation. Just who did he think he was, to speak to her like that? To make matters worse, the fact that he'd addressed her in English suggested he'd overheard her own personal rebuke. How embarrassing!

With a couple of easy strides he was beside her, grabbing hold of her wrist and almost dragging her back into the dim light of the building. Alison tried to shrug off his grasp, but to no avail. His grip on her wrist was like clamped steel.

'And before you scream rape, forget it. I don't go in for scrawny schoolgirls.' Hooded eyes raked her slender form dismissively while Alison spluttered like a stranded fish, too outraged even to attempt an answer. Scrawny schoolgirl! How dared he insult and manhandle her like this?

As soon as they reached the shower block's entrance, she wrenched her wrist from his grip with deliberate vehemence and then felt a little foolish when he released it so easily. Nevertheless she rubbed it conspicuously and glanced up at him, partly in defiance, partly wary. There had been a threatening aura about him in the shadows which wasn't diminished greatly even in the light. His facial features were obscured, but nothing could disguise the ruggedness of his frame. Over six foot in height and powerfully built, the overall impression was one of overt masculinity. Dark clothing—either black or navy—she couldn't be sure which—added to his stern, forbidding aspect.

'Who are you, and what the hell do you think you're doing here at this time of night?' he demanded roughly.

After his peremptory manner of introduction, Alison hardly expected cordiality, but all the same the terse brusqueness of his tone took her by surprise. He might not be a rapist, but he was an ill-mannered brute none the less.

'I could ask you the same question,' she replied curtly, managing to sound cool despite a degree of trepidation. He didn't look the sort of man to barter questions kindly.

The man gave a husky, humourless chuckle. 'You could, except I'm asking the questions and I'm waiting for an answer.'

The sheer arrogance of his tone and manner made Alison want to kick his shins, but the schoolgirl

reference still irked. She didn't like being called a
schoolgirl, still less being treated like one, and she
was damn sure he wasn't going to make her behave
like one. Nor was she going to stand here and answer
his questions like an errant pupil brought before the
headmaster. He might have delusions of power, but
she had no intention of concurring with them. 'That's
nothing to do with you, and I refuse to stand here
debating the point.' She turned to go, indicating that
as far as she was concerned their conversation, if that
was the right word for it, was at at end.

The hand falling on her shoulder detained her, not
forcefully but purposefully, making it quite clear that
he didn't intend to be thwarted.

She swung round. 'I warn you, I can scream very
loudly.'

'I know. I just heard you,' he acknowledged drily.
And then released her to slide his hand into his
trouser-pocket in a deceptively casual gesture,
offering, 'Go on. Scream away.'

Alison could have sworn she saw his lips curve in
faint amusement. Damn him, he was calling her
bluff. He knew as well as she did that they were too
far from the centre for her screams to be heard. There
was nothing amusing about all this from her point of
view. Who was this man? And, if he did have any
menacing intent towards her, what on earth could
she do out here, beyond even hearing-range? A
cursory glance was all it took to confirm that she
would be no match for his powerful physique.
Unconsciously she edged away from him. If she
couldn't fight, then she could at least make a run for
it.

The man crooked an elbow against the wooden structure of the porch-style entrance and raked his fingers through dark, almost black hair in a gesture of impatience, as if her thought processes had been blatantly transparent. 'Look, all I want to know is who you are and what you're doing here.'

Sometimes honesty was the best means of defence, Alison observed resignedly. Perhaps if she simply answered his questions, irksome though it was to have to do so, he would leave her alone.

'Not that I consider it to be any of your business . . . but I happen to be one of the Summer Canvas couriers,' she informed him through gritted teeth, piqued by the necessity of a volte-face on her part.

Another assessing glance from those hooded eyes, clearly no more complimentary than the first. '*Bien Dieu* . . . You girls get younger every year. You're sure you're out of school?'

'Quite sure,' she retorted crisply, irritated almost beyond words by his derisive assessment. Had this man never heard of tact, let alone charm? And she'd always believed the French were famous for it. 'And now, if you've quite finished——' She paused. He wasn't going to get the chance to restrain her physically again.

'And what are you doing up here?' the man persisted, eyes narrowed almost suspiciously.

This really was too much. 'Taking a shower. Any objections?' Faced with such provocation, an insolent drawl crept into Alison's voice.

The man grinned, revealing even, white teeth, and his eyes sauntered lazily downwards. 'None whatsoever. But why up here? Why not at one of the shower blocks nearer the centre?'

Good lord! What did this man want? An alibi? Had a murder been committed? Her own eyes narrowed, their brown depths becoming slits of glinting anger. 'Because this is the *first*, and *only*, shower block to have been the plumbing reconnected. I don't know why the plumbers started with the block furthest from the centre. It's French logic. *You* ask them.' Her voice rose to a tight-lipped crescendo. If he asked her just one more inane question, she swore she'd scream. If only to relieve her frustration.

But finally he seemed satisfied. She sensed rather than saw a relaxing of the taut muscles and sinews beneath the jacket he was wearing, and his face lost some of its harsh tension, the lines around his eyes and mouth easing into something approaching a smile. He looked like a man who smiled a lot—in the right mood. But Alison didn't care about his moods and she certainly wasn't in any mood to reciprocate his affability now, not after the grilling he'd just given her.

'But why the scream?' he queried after a pause, as if it were an afterthought.

'Pardon?' Alison had almost forgotten how this encounter had begun.

'You screamed, remember?' he reminded her with dry patience.

'Oh . . . er . . . that.' Alison frowned, embarrassed now to recall her reaction to one small bat. 'It was a . . . er . . . bat.'

'A bat, hmm?' The man raised an eyebrow with faint cynicism.

All the time she was standing, Alison felt herself

getting colder and colder. Her damp hair clung to her scalp and rats' tails allowed trickles of water to drip under the neckline of her sweatshirt and down her back, making her shiver. What was she doing here, offering explanations to a complete stranger who had no business whatsoever asking her questions and who then had the affront to doubt the answers he'd forced out of her? 'Yes, a bat,' she affirmed tersely. Hard luck if he didn't believe her. And she turned resolutely away from him, determined this time to brook no restraint. He'd had his answers; let him chew them and spit them out if they didn't suit.

'I'll walk with you . . .' surprisingly, the man fell into step beside her '. . . just in case any more bats take aim at you,' he added, making a mockery of any gallant intention.

Alison wanted to strike him, kick him, anything to be rid of him, but she stared rigidly ahead, refusing to allow such childish impulses to get the better of her. So blinkered was her vision that she was totally unprepared for his next action. The man took off his jacket and swung it casually round her shoulders. Immediately she tried to shrug it off. 'It's not necessary . . .' she began, but the man interrupted, more gently this time.

'Don't be foolish, you're obviously cold. Besides, I don't want one of the couriers coming down with pneumonia.' The soft mockery made it sound like self-interest rather than concern and, faced with such indifference, Alison abandoned the unseemly struggle to remove the jacket.

The quilted material did indeed warm her, but more compelling to her senses was the potent mascu-

line aroma which clung to it. It reminded her
uncomfortably of Jonathon. She wanted to hurry up
and be rid of the memories it conjured . . . and the
man. Unconsciously she quickened her footsteps, but
the man merely lengthened his stride and kept pace
easily beside her. When they reached the triangle
where the pathway met the road, she slid the jacket
off hurriedly and handed it to him with a grudging
thank you. Then, without even giving him a chance
to reply, she turned quickly away and headed in the
direction of her tent.

As the first stealthy fingers of daylight penetrated the
green canvas, Alison's eyes opened drowsily and she
turned over to try to ease herself into a marginally
more comfortable position on the narrow camp-bed.
But it was no good, a month's use had made the bed
no more accommodating than it had been on the first
night, and Alison gave a rueful smile as she
wondered whether, at the end of six months, a divan
would seem as strange as this bed had done on their
first night here.

  The courier's job with Summer Canvas had been
Jane's idea. She'd worked for them, at this same site,
the previous year, and had enjoyed it so much that
she'd applied again. A couple of months ago, the
idea of joining her would not even have occurred to
Alison, much less appealed. But, presenting itself
when it did, the opportunity had seemed an
incredible stroke of luck. The courier originally
assigned to this site with Jane had broken her leg in a
skiing accident, and the company were desperate to
find a replacement at short notice. Although Alison

had no experience of this type of work, her languages background had compensated and she'd handed in her notice at work and signed the Summer Canvas contract almost without drawing breath.

Understandably, her mother had been aghast. 'A holiday I could understand . . . but a camp-site . . . for six months . . . darling, you don't know what you're doing!' Useless to try and explain. Her mother's mind ran along well-trammelled lines, and the whole notion of her daughter giving up a good, secure job with an international legal company for the transient, gypsy-like existence of a camp-site courier was inconceivable to her. And all for the sake of a mere male! But Alison was not to be swayed. Like an animal spotting a bolt-hole, she'd bulldozed ahead with her plans.

Through the flimsy material which separated their sleeping compartments, Alison could just make out Jane's still form slumbering peacefully beneath a voluminous orange blanket. Stirring quietly so as not to disturb her sleeping friend, she detached herself from her sleeping-bag and crept across to the corner of the tent where her clothes lay discarded from the night before.

With stealthy movements she pulled them on and then picked up her toilet-bag and towel, moving furtively across to release the noisy zip of the door flap. Expectantly she held her breath, but no protesting sounds of arousal came from Jane's corner.

It was a glorious morning, full of promise for the day ahead and indeed the rest of the summer. Cotton-wool clouds hung negligently in the sky, white balls of fluff against an azure blue. Alison leaned against the fence running alongside their tent and surveyed the acres of greenery stretching into the distance. When they'd first arrived, this view had been uninterrupted by signs of civilisation. It had symbolised the heart of rural Dordogne, green and languid, bordered by deep wooded areas of deciduous oak, ash, birch and beech. Occasionally foxes, squirrels and rabbits would sprint across it, vivid specks of movement on its peaceful expanse. But now the same area was chequered with multicoloured tents, many sporting the distinctive green and yellow logo of Summer Canvas. Other colours represented Summer Canvas's competitors, who also retained sites here. The tents stretched across the whole area, just as if a gingham cloth had been spread over it, deserted now but quietly anticipating the arrival of hundreds of couples and families by the weekend.

The site had taken as its hub the original farm buildings and converted them to accommodate the amenities necessary for a large, modern camp-site: food shops, restaurants, bar, disco, launderette, first-aid centre, even a swimming pool complex. The inclusion of more modern buildings in with the traditional ochre-coloured limestone ones had been skilfully done so that much of the setting's original charm remained, though its function had changed considerably.

It was towards this central area that Alison now headed. The whole centre had the appearance of a ghost town waiting to be peopled. It would not have to wait long; the fifteenth of May, the official opening day, was now less than a week away, and there were abundant signs of the preparations being made for it: fresh paint, new signs, everywhere pristine-clean and bright.

In the deserted washroom, Alison stood before one of the basins and set her soap-bag and towel on the tiled ledge beside her. It was a large room, accommodating some ten wash-basins along each wall, with individual shower-type curtains providing the means for privacy if desired. She turned on the cold water tap; there was no point in turning on the hot since it hadn't been reconnected in here yet. This spartan washing arrangement had been the norm for the last month—that was what had made last night's shower such an enjoyable luxury. Or at least, it had been until that awful man had come along with his rudeness and boorish behaviour. Schoolgirl, indeed!

The flannel in her hand paused mid-way to her face and Alison regarded herself critically in the oval mirror above the basin. At twenty-four, she didn't find being mistaken for a schoolgirl in the least complimentary. Did she really look so gauche . . . so unfeminine? That was what his appraisal had implied.

Deep button-brown eyes fringed with dark lashes stared back at her above a gently uptilted nose and wide, generous lips. Nothing unfeminine there, she averred defensively. Her hair . . . well, her hair, that was another matter. Even after six weeks it still looked strange when she glanced in a mirror or felt its quick release when she pulled a comb through it. The long mass of auburn-coloured tresses had always been her 'crowning glory', as her mother had proudly referred to it, and probably her most

feminine feature. But six weeks ago, without
consulting anyone, she'd had it cut as short as
possible. A symbolic gesture, a new beginning after
Jonathon, she'd told herself. It hadn't suited her,
even she'd had to admit it in the end. But it was
starting to grow again now and the soft, curling
tendrils were beginning to take away the harshness
of that first brutal cut. Perhaps last night, bereft of
make-up and with hair plastered to her scalp, she had
looked somewhat . . . immature. Maybe his
assessment could be excused, but definitely—very
definitely—not his abominable manner. Her pert
nose wrinkling in distaste at the memory, Alison
finished washing and then brushed her teeth with a
zeal her dentist would have been proud of.

On her way back to the tent, Alison took a different
route, one that would take her alongside the grounds
of the château. It was one of her favourite walks, and
she never tired of observing the magnificent building.
Camp Belreynac took its site and name from the
château, but the château itself remained a separate
entity, with its privacy intact. Alison surveyed its
grandeur from a slight rise just beyond the far side of
the central complex. Built in the same yellow stone as
the original farm buildings, it rose up in a great
golden mass, glowering over the landscape for miles
around. Its dormer windows, corbels, mansards,
turrets and weather vanes gave it an enchanting
fairy-tale quality, and Alison often tried to imagine its
history and the family secrets hidden behind the
fortress-like walls. Her eyes searched now for signs of
movement, but found none. Apart from the
gardeners she'd seen no sign of life there, and its

occupants—if indeed it was occupied— intrigued her. She must remember to ask Jane about it, she chivvied herself as she started walking again in the direction of the tent.

Nine-thirty a.m. and Alison surveyed the mountains of crockery and cutlery waiting to be rinsed and dried with spunky determination. Five hundred dishes, plates, cups, saucers, glasses, knives, forks, spoons and goodness knew what else. What a Herculean task! Resolutely she pulled on bright orange rubber gloves and thrust her hands into the soapy liquid.

Her mother would have a fit if she could see her now, Alison decided with a rueful smile. Was this what the extra years at secretarial college had led to? Was this what her daughter had given up a good, well-paid job for? It was true that this last month had been a complete contrast to her previous job as personal secretary to the managing director of Legate and Barker International. There her work had been mentally stimulating, demanding . . . enjoyable too, but it certainly hadn't prepared her in any way for the sheer hard physical work involved in being a camp-site courier.

The last month had been spent erecting tents. Summer Canvas employed a team to travel to all their sites across Europe during April and May, erecting anywhere between fifty and a hundred tents at each site, assisted by the couriers. At the beginning of the month, Alison had hardly known one end of a tent from another; by the end she felt she could have erected them in her sleep.

It was tiring work but she hadn't minded that,

almost welcomed it in fact. There'd been little time to deliberate and brood, and at night she fell immediately into a dreamless sleep, the restlessness of her mind overcome by the sheer physical exhaustion of her body. Amazing how intense physical employment could take control of your life, giving it a routine and discipline which simply carried it along, edging out all unnecessary activities—even thinking. She still thought about Jonathon, of course. It would have been impossible not to. But his total dominance of all her waking hours had ceased, and she was grateful for it.

Now she tackled the washing-up with resignation while Jane took herself off to inflate air-beds, yet another of the seemingly endless list of tasks to be completed before the camp officially opened.

At lunch time Jane appeared in the doorway bearing a *baguette* and cheese. 'I reckoned you could muster up some plates and knives,' she grinned, glancing wryly towards the ever-increasing tower of plates and piles of cutlery on the drainer.

'Just about,' Alison agreed, smiling and peeling off the rubber gloves with some relief.

Outside, the two of them sat down on the grassy bank and cut off lengths of bread and chunks of cheese. A somewhat primitive picnic, but appetising none the less. Why did food eaten outdoors always taste so much better? Alison wondered, biting into a crispy hunk of bread.

'How are the air-beds?' she queried between mouthfuls.

Jane raised her eyes in mock horror. 'Don't ask. Even with a foot-pump those things take for ever to inflate. I reckon we should tell the visitors it's an activity holiday and let them do their own.'

Alison laughed out loud, imagining people's expressions if they did any such thing. Jane had been so good for her these last few weeks. Her buoyant manner and zany brand of humour had contributed as much as anything to helping her get over Jonathon. If, indeed, she was over him. Did you ever really get over loving someone and having to accept that they didn't love you in return? At the moment she didn't have the answer to that poser; all she did know was that life had once again assumed moments of humour, of light-hearted relief, even pleasure, compared with the totally black abyss of only a couple of months ago. For the moment that was enough. 'One hurdle at a time' had always been her mother's motto, and now, despite its trite simplicity, she was finding some truth in the words.

'What else is there left to do?' she asked. 'Assuming I ever do get through that lot,' nodding in the direction of the dishwashing area.

'Don't ask,' Jane advised, shaking her head with exaggerated solemnity. 'There's all the equipment to check yet . . . cookers, cool-boxes, tables, chairs, barbecues, plus all sorts of little fiddly things. But,' she added, more cheerfully, 'it should be all right. We had to check everything before putting it into storage at the end of last season so, in theory, it should all be in working order.'

Alison raised a cynical eyebrow. She knew all about the wide gap between theory and practice, but no doubt it would all get done somehow between now and Saturday. Lying back on the grass, she closed her

eyes; the sun was warm and balmy on her eyelids
and a soft breeze ruffled her hair. It really would be
very easy to just drift off to sleep and forget about the
preparations altogether, pretend you were just
another visitor come here to relax and enjoy yourself.
Only a low, appreciative whistle from Jane roused
her and made her open one eye enquiringly.

'Not bad,' Jane murmured admiringly.

Alison propped herself up on her elbows and
glanced in the direction Jane was staring. A sleek,
low-slung sports car with tinted windows was
cruising slowly along the approach road towards the
site.

'Nice car,' Alison murmured indifferently, and
flopped back on to the grass.

'Even nicer owner,' Jane specified emphatically.

Alison vaguely wondered whether her own
eyesight had become deficient or whether Jane had
suddenly developed X-ray vision. She hadn't been
able to see a thing through the tinted glass. 'How can
you tell?' she queried with drowsy curiosity.

'I'd know that car anywhere. It belongs to Comte
Belreynac,' Jane declared with some satisfaction.

That piece of information prompted a more
interested response. 'Who? You mean the owner of
the château?'

'The château *and* the camp-site. Both,' Jane
emphasised. 'He must be here for the summer
season.'

Alison sat up again but by now the car had disappeared from sight, leaving only a trail of rising dust
in its wake. So, the château did have an owner.

'What's he like?' Alison wondered, trying to

imagine the French equivalent of an English country gentleman with shooting stick and tweeds.

'Gorgeous, single and very, very eligible,' Jane summed him up in her own inimitably moderate manner, completely dispelling the image of shooting sticks and tweeds.

'Oh!' Alison responded abstrusely, at the same time deciding she wasn't very interested in the château's owner, after all. Gorgeous single men, only too well aware of their own attractions and eligibility, were no longer her scene, she'd decided. Not after Jonathon. She'd had enough of the heart-hammering, emotional big-dipper relationships to last a lifetime. Fine for those few brief moments when you hit the top, but absolute hell when you plunged downwards again.

With a sigh of resignation as she mentally envisaged the piles of dishes still to be rinsed, she changed the subject. 'Hadn't we better get back to work?'

Jane grimaced. 'I guess you're right. We can't have the visitors sleeping on the ground and eating with their fingers.'

Standing up and brushing the breadcrumbs off her clothes, Alison gathered together the plates and knives they'd used and headed back towards the dishwashing area, pausing only to give Jane a quick wave as she set off in the opposite direction.

When they returned to their tent early in the evening, a piece of paper had been pushed under the door-flap. It was an invitation from the site manager inviting them, and the other couriers, to join him and the Comte in the bar for drinks that evening.

Alison sighed inwardly. She'd been quietly looking forward to another hot shower, hopefully without the rude stranger this time, and an early night. A social gathering, however informal, had not been on the agenda. 'Do we have to go?' she protested half to herself.

Jane's shocked expression confirmed the answer. 'Of course we have to go . . . the Comte's expecting us . . . it would be extremely rude not to turn up. Besides, you want to meet him, don't you?'

While reluctantly accepting that Jane's first points were probably correct, Alison wasn't at all sure about the last. She knew next to nothing about the Comte, but what she did know didn't appeal. Not in the least. Perhaps Jonathon had jaundiced her whole attitude to men, in particular single, attractive, eligible ones. Just as when you eat a particular type of shellfish and are ill afterwards, you somehow don't want to risk them again. But, whatever her private thoughts on the matter, the Comte was the owner of the site. It probably wouldn't be very diplomatic to offend him by refusing his invitation, and once she'd put in an appearance she could always make some excuse and leave early.

'You're right,' she conceded, 'it would be rude not to go.'

Jane looked relieved and immediately leapt into action, more concerned now with what to wear. 'Oh, God! I haven't anything decent to put on. All my dresses are crumpled and I haven't even got a clean pair of trousers.'

Alison regarded her with some surprise. 'What's the fuss? It's only an informal get-together, not the annual ball.'

But Jane continued to ransack holdalls and rucksacks. 'You haven't met *him*.'

The *him* could only be the Comte. The manager was a familiar figure round the site, and for all his pleasant good humour, his plump, middle-aged frame was not likely to quicken any maiden's heartbeat. No, *he* had to be the Comte, and Jane's awed tone immediately conjured up images of autocratic ogres from European fairy-tales. Powerful, but never very sympathetic characters.

Alison refused to be fazed by the invitation. What could the man expect when they lived in a tent and hadn't had the use of a washing machine, let alone an iron, for over a month, Determined to dress casually, she drew out a pair of white midi-length jeans and a blue and white striped T-shirt. She almost reached for the baggy sweatshirt from yesterday evening, but then decided against it. That scrawny schoolgirl reference still nettled. Instead she chose a white cotton cardigan and knotted it round her shoulders.

'Why don't hot buttered croissants have any effect on your figure?' Jane paused in her rummaging and eyed Alison's slender frame with just a shade of envy.

Alison bent down to slip on a pair of flat-heeled sandals. 'I was accused of being scrawny yesterday—that's not much of a compliment.'

Fortunately Jane didn't stop to ponder on who had made the remark, simply assuming it had been a man, and, turning back to her open suitcase, only muttered darkly, 'Men, there's no pleasing them. Why do we bother?'

It was a question Alison had often asked herself recently, and she hadn't been able to come up with an answer, but Jane seemed content to let the rhetorical question hang in the air and continued to rummage as furiously as before.

After several changes, she finally selected a seersucker skirt on the grounds that the material would look as if it was meant to be crumpled, and a T-shirt which really needed ironing but the creases of which disappeared when stretched across Jane's ample bosom.

'Just one advantage of buying T-shirts a size too small,' Jane grinned, and winked so wickedly that Alison dared not ask what the others were.

CHAPTER TWO

THIS was the first opportunity they'd had to visit the bar. As with all the other facilities, it had lain dormant under a winter cloak of dust-sheets and shutters, emerging now spruced up and newly furbished for the summer season, Converted from one of the original barns, it had been decorated in a deliberately rustic style, with the rough-hewn stone walls and ancient roof timbers exposed. Antiquated farm implements and sepia photographs of bygone days adorned the walls, yet an air of modern intimacy had been introduced with the subdued lighting and alcove seating arrangements, cleverly using wrought-iron dividers removed from the old stables.

At the entrance they were greeted by the site manager, looking as spruce as the setting in a smart new suit stretched taut across his middle, and neatly combed hair, carefully arranged to camouflage its sparsity. Alison smiled affectionately at the small touches of vanity; he was a nice man, helpful and friendly. Obligingly she pinned the name badge he handed over on to her T-shirt and progressed into the centre of the room.

About twenty people were already gathered there, some full-time site workers, and others couriers from rival holiday companies. Their employers might have been rivals, but it was not a term which occurred to the couriers to use about themselves. A great deal of friendly camaraderie existed between them, and most were more than willing to help others out in times of difficulty.

After helping themselves to glasses of white wine at the bar, Jane went over to join Simon and Matthew, who occupied the neighbouring tent to their own, and Alison deliberately went to talk to David and Helen. So far, she'd found these two the least approachable, particularly David. Like Jane, he'd worked at the site the previous year and tended to adopt a brash, independent air which set him apart and could be irksome. But Alison liked Helen and sensed she sometimes felt divided loyalties, wanting to support David because they worked together, yet enjoying the relaxed informality of the other couriers and wanting to make friends with them, too.

'You received a summons, too,' she jested by way of greeting, and then, because she had to admit to a mild degree of curiosity, 'Is the Comte here yet?' She knew David would recognise him from last year.

David glanced round uninterestedly. 'No.' The curt response did not invite further conversation and Helen shifted uncomfortably, staring down into her glass.

'Are you ready for the first visitors?' Alison tried again.

'Just about,' David admitted stiffly.

'How about you?' Helen interjected quickly, sensing David's cool indifference and trying to compensate for it.

Alison grimaced. 'Let's just say I don't want to see another plastic beaker for at least a week, and Jane says she's inflated so many air-beds today that her feet will be pumping up and down in her sleep.'

Helen laughed, but David remained as po-faced as ever, his face looking as if it would crack if so much as a glimmer of a smile rippled its immobile features.

Blow him, Alison thought crossly, he's such a cold fish that nothing would amuse him.

An empty silence descended between the three of them, with David clearly determined not to fill it and Helen not daring to. Alison drained her glass, intending to make her excuses and join the others, but David beat her to it.

'If you don't mind, I do have some things to discuss with Helen . . . in private.'

'Not at all.' Alison smiled sweetly. 'I've always been able to take a hint, especially when it's dropped so heavily.'

She did at least have the satisfaction of seeing David colour slightly, but it was Helen who blushed scarlet. Poor thing, Alison thought as she turned away, I don't envy her having to work with him all summer.

A finger-food buffet was set out at one end of the room and, since couriers, like students, never said no to a free meal, that was where the group was clustered. Alison joined in the friendly chatter with some relief after David's blunt rudeness and, looking along the table, surveyed the attractive spread. Picking up something long and crispy-looking, she crunched it between her teeth. It didn't in the least resemble the spicy flavour she had been anticipating, and when visions of legless frogs began to float through her mind she hastily helped herself to another glass of wine to drown the taste.

In the background one record stopped and another started. An old Diana Ross single. The words were in French, but it didn't matter. The English version was engraved in Alison's memory. It had been one of Jonathon's favourites and she tensed as the familiar words and melody sounded across the room. Her throat constricted horribly and tears pricked the backs of her eyelids. She and Jonathon had listened, laughed, loved, to that music. That was when she had thought Jonathon would be part of all her tomorrows, that he would fill her life, never allowing it to be empty again. Why shouldn't it have lasted for ever?

With too brittle a smile and too loud a laugh, she responded to a joke Simon had just made and then, before anyone could see through the shallow act, moved quickly away from the group, ostensibly to examine one of the photographs on the far wall.

She peered at it, not seeing it through a blur of tears, and then swung round in shocked surprise as a voice she recognised sounded behind her.

'Good evening.' That French accent was unmistakable.

Oh, no! The man of the previous evening. That was all she needed.

'Good evening,' she replied curtly and turned back quickly, furiously blinking back her tears, fingers tightening on the round glass.

'You like old photographs?'

Alison nodded fiercely, without looking at him. 'Fascinated by them,' she declared emphatically, hoping her desire for solitude and lack of company, his in particular, would be obvious.

Some hope! His next words horrified her.

'Perhaps you could study it better if it were the right way up.' The words were bland enough but there was no mistaking the mocking undertone.

'Pardon . . .' Alison began, not immediately understanding his meaning, and looking blankly from him to the picture as he reached forward, removed it from its hook and turned it the right way up. Clearly, in hasty last-minute preparations, someone had inadvertently hung the picture upside-down. She hadn't even noticed.

'Or is it maybe an English hobby I am unaware of, studying upside-down pictures?' This time there was no attempt to disguise the mockery.

In desperation Alison took another gulp of the wine and began to choke. 'I must need glasses,' she spluttered lamely, wondering just how much he'd seen and what interpretation he'd put on it. The humour in his tone had been evident but not unkind. Coughing disguised her earlier tears, and for the first time she dared look at him properly, nothing wrong with her eyesight now. Dressed as he was in casual dark trousers and a white open-necked shirt which exposed a hint of bronzed flesh and dark curling chest hair beneath, the vibrant aura of masculinity she had experienced last night was no less potent in this indoor setting. A lamp on the wall highlighted the features of his face, all hard planes and angles; square chin, chiselled lips, straight nose. Only his eyes, a most unusual green in colour, relieved the impression of harsh virility, but even they, Alison sensed, would have the cold indifference of the sea in moments of anger. His hair wasn't as dark as she had thought, mahogany rather than ebony, and it just touched his collar, neither too long nor too short. About thirty-three or thirty-four? She tried to estimate his age.

Alison hadn't appreciated the baldness of her scrutiny, perhaps because, although she recognised his obvious attractions as a male, she had no personal interest in them. It was a dispassionate examination of the species, and not until she caught a glimpse of amusement in the raised eyebrow and curled lip did she realise her error. For error it most definitely was. Without a word being exchanged between them, it was clear that he intended to redress the balance.

His eyes began a slow, deliberate descent, assessing every curve with exaggerated interest, just as she must have seemed to do. Alison debated whether to throw the rest of the wine in his face or drink it, as if oblivious to his scrutiny. Restraint won and she tipped the glass, allowing the last drops of cool liquid to trickle down her throat. When his eyes returned to hers, there was at least some satisfaction in his silent acknowledgement that the schoolgirl label of the night before had well and truly been dispelled.

However, when his eyes returned with indecent haste to a particular area of her anatomy, Alison wondered whether the moment *had* come to slap his face. Redressing the balance was one thing, overloading the scales something else altogether. Just in time, she realised he was only reading the name badge pinned to her chest.

'Alison Taylor.' The name rolled off his tongue in

a very French manner, and then, 'How very English.'

Alison felt like hitting him. 'What's yours?' she enquired sweetly. Did she detect a glimmer of a smile in anticipation of her attack?

'Maximilien.'

Alison smiled innocently. 'How *very* French.'

The man—she couldn't possibly think of him as Maximilien—chuckled.

'*Touché* . . . or should it be touchy?'

Alison couldn't be sure whether he was genuinely uncertain of the pun or whether he was deliberately making fun of her. Those green eyes gave nothing away.

'*Touché* is fine,' she averred firmly.

'You're not touchy, then?' Now his eyes glinted with humour.

Damn him and his fluent English. 'Not at all,' she shrugged dismissively, refusing even to consider how much he might have read into her actions earlier. Her state of mind was none of his business. But hadn't she thought the very same thing yesterday about his questions, and hadn't he persevered until he'd made it his business? She wouldn't allow the same thing to happen again. Making a faint movement towards him, she indicated her intention of rejoining the rest of her group. But, instead of moving aside as she expected, the man leaned back against one of the alcove dividers, casually yet very effectively blocking her passage. Any attempt to get past him would put them into impossible proximity. For the moment she stood her ground.

He smiled negligently. 'That's good. I thought you

might still be nettled by our encounter last night.'

Alison opened her eyes wide in mock surprise. 'Really? I don't know why. You only yelled at me, bullied me and manhandled me. Why should I be annoyed?'

'I had my reasons.' It was a curt statement, making it clear that, whatever his reasons were, he wasn't going to explain them.

'I'm glad to hear it,' Alison conceded drily. 'I'd hate to think you behaved like that for fun.'

This time he laughed out loud, his eyes flicking over her with shrewd interest. 'For fun . . . I haven't heard that expression in a long time. No, Miss Taylor, that's certainly not what I do *for fun.*'

His emphasis on the words suddenly shifted the conversation into whole new territory, and Alison shifted uncomfortably in awareness of it. Licking her lips in an unconsciously provocative gesture, she observed gravely, 'How very reassuring.'

His eyes held hers. 'Do you need reassurance?' he asked softly, sexily, making the perfectly innocuous word sound positively debauched.

Two glasses of wine had made Alison feel more relaxed, and now she wasn't sure whether to feel offended or amused by the sexual undercurrents threading their conversation. 'Only when low-flying bats take aim at me,' she offered with mock solemnity, playing him at his own game.

He chuckled. 'I must admit that was a very loud scream. You probably frightened the poor creature to death.'

She shrugged. 'I was just practising in case there was anything more ferocious around . . . like wolves.'

'Didn't you know there are no wild ones left in France?'

Alison smiled pertly. 'Who said I was referring to the animal variety?'

The man smiled back lazily. 'After that scream I'd have thought either variety would be wary of you.'

Alison wasn't at all sure it was a compliment— after all, it hadn't deterred him—nevertheless she smiled gravely. 'Thank you.'

'You're not a fan of wolves, or men, then?'

This conversation was getting decidedly sticky, and Alison was no longer totally sure of its direction. She didn't like not feeling in control, but then she got the feeling this man . . . Maximilien . . . didn't either.

'I don't mind them in zoos,' she answered ambiguously, a slight smile playing on her lips despite her fears. Verbal semantics could be fun as long as the topics remained impersonal. It was one of the things she missed about Jonathon—that and a hundred other things. Both of them lively-minded and intelligent, they'd argued, debated, discussed everything together, from nuclear power to test-tube babies. She'd thought it was a sign of their compatibility. Why hadn't Jonathon thought so, too?

'Pardon?'

The man's voice brought her back to the present and she shook her head impatiently to dismiss Jonathon's image.

'I said is that what the feminists would do . . . put us in cages?' A smile hovered on his lips and, as Alison's eyes ranged again over his powerful frame, it wasn't difficult to understand what prompted his amusement. What woman could get him into a cage against his will?

'Only some,' she murmured, half aware of her thoughts drifting again to Jonathon. That was what he'd said, something like that, in those bitter final words between them. *You want to chain me, tie me down. I don't belong to you.* No, you couldn't cage people. If they didn't choose to remain with you of their own free will, then you had to let them go.

She became aware of the man watching her intently, his expression inscrutable. 'Some people build cages round themselves to keep what they fear at bay.'

Brown eyes flashed defensively. What was he trying to say? He was far too personal for her liking. Personal where she was concerned at least; he didn't like the process in reverse. He made it clear that his own affairs were private, so what made him think he could pry into hers? 'What an interesting observation,' she remarked, sarcasm edging her voice like a knife-blade. 'I didn't realise amateur psychology was another of your talents.'

'It isn't,' he conceded smoothly,' but it doesn't take a psychologist to see that you're bristling like a hedgehog. Look.' And without warning he reached out and brushed her forearm with his fingers. She flinched as if he had hit her. 'See?' He levelled the evidence against her.

If they hadn't been in such a public place, Alison knew she would have hit him. As it was, her knuckles whitened as they gripped her empty glass. The rough feel of his fingers grazing her skin angered her almost as much as his behaviour last night. No, more. Last night his behaviour had at least been spontaneous—primitive, but spontaneous. Now his touch had been deliberately provocative, as if she were part of some scientific experiment. 'How dare you?' she hissed through clenched teeth. 'What the hell gives you the right to such arrogant presumptuousness? I'm not a slab of meat on a butcher's block, and in future I'd prefer you to keep your hands and your opinions to yourself.'

The man's features hardened like molten metal setting in a mould, becoming flinty and inflexible; only his eyes betrayed movement, flickering over her disdainfully. 'What was that I said about bristles? You haven't got bristles, you're covered in spikes. I'd get that name badge changed if I were you, to something more appropriate, like Alison the Untouchable.'

This time when Alison went to move, the man deliberately moved aside, as if to practically demonstrate the force of his final words. Head high, she moved away from him, refusing to hurry, though every instinct told her to put as much distance between them as possible.

On the far side of the room, Jane was signalling furiously and Alison headed straight towards her.

'What's the matter?' she asked as soon as she reached her, glad to be able to focus on Jane rather than have to deflect any awkward questions.

Jane fanned her flushed cheeks with a paper plate. 'I've been trying to catch your eye for ages . . . do you realise . . .'

At that moment a loud knocking sounded at the other end of the room and the site manager called for everyone's attention. 'Many of you already know

Comte Belreynac, but, for those newcomers this year, please let me introduce him.'

A dark figure made his way down to that end of the room and Alison gave a hushed gasp as she recognised him . . . Oh, no! It couldn't be . . . Comte *Maximilien* Belreynac.

His speech made little impact on Alison. She hardly heard any of it in the flurry of thoughts that whistled round her mind. What would happen now? Would she be expelled like an errant schoolgirl for speaking insolently to the head? Sent home in disgrace? Don't be ridiculous, she told herself firmly. He has no authority to dismiss you . . . you're employed by Summer Canvas and, as long as you do your job properly, he has no jurisdiction over you. But the arguments inside her head persisted right through his speech. She heard nothing of it. But what did that matter? Regardless of what words of welcome and encouragement he extended to other newcomers, how could any of them apply to her? Among all the couriers on the site, she must be the only one who had managed to anger and antagonise the owner, not once, but twice, within twenty-four hours. The fact that it was entirely mutual seemed somehow irrelevant at the moment.

CHAPTER THREE

ON SATURDAY the first batch of visitors arrived and there was no time to think in the rush to direct people to their tents, explain where various amenities were situated and answer a miscellaneous assortment of questions ranging in complexity from the best places in the area for fishing to how one asked for an ice-cream in French.

By the end of the day, Alison was exhausted. Her mind and body felt as if they had been pulled in too many directions and finally snapped. As she flopped back on to a lounger outside their tent, Jane regarded her sympathetically. 'It's always worst the first couple of days . . . everyone's so keen to get on and enjoy their holiday, they want to know everything at once. And the courier is expected to be the miracle worker with all the answers.'

Alison didn't feel very much like a miracle worker at the moment; in fact she felt more than a little in need of a miracle herself. Ever since the evening in the bar and the discovery that Maximilien was the owner of Camp Belreynac, she'd oscillated between anxiety over her position here and indifference to whatever action—if any—he chose to take. After all, there were only so many ways you could get fired! She'd expected him to make some sort of approach— demand an apology, her resignation, something!

But there'd been no word and no sight of him either. Uncertainty had made the situation worse and had caused a curious feeling of apprehension to hang over her for the rest of the week. Now, with the lapse of time, she felt reasonably confident that no action would be taken, but nevertheless the doubts had taken their toll and, after a day like today, of being consistently bright, cheerful and helpful, she felt drained of all emotion.

It wasn't like her to be such a worrier, so assailed by doubts. She'd always prided herself on being decisive and strong-minded; her self-assurance had been a major factor in acquiring promotion at such an early age to personal secretary to the managing director. But after what happened with Jonathon—the sudden realisation that her judgement, her trust, had been so badly misplaced—self-confidence and self-esteem hit rock bottom. Over here, far removed from that life, from Jonathon, a natural process of healing and rebuilding had begun. Everything had been going so well until that man, Comte Belreynac, came on the scene with his intrusive conundrums. Good lord, the man was arrogant! Alison closed her eyes against his image, knowing as she did so that it was a futile exercise. How could she visually block out something already so clearly imprinted on her mind?

Technically Sunday was a quiet day for the couriers. Once they had delivered ice-packs for cool boxes and English newspapers, their time—in theory—was their own. Inevitably, it didn't work out quite like that in practice. Especially not since this was the first Sunday of the season. There was still a host of minor tasks to be dealt with, overlapping from the day before and, understandably, because they had only just arrived themselves, visitors still came to ask for directions, translations and a whole range of other queries. By lunch time Jane had had enough. 'I'm going off site for a couple of hours,' she announced firmly, 'and I'd advise you to do the same if you want to get any peace. Why don't you come into Sarlat with me?'

Alison recognised the sense of the suggestion, but didn't feel in the mood for mixing with throngs of tourists. Since it was close enough to the site to be reached by bicycle, they'd already visited Sarlat on a number of occasions. It was a lovely old market town and a delight to explore with its narrow, winding streets and medieval architecture, but she knew that today it would be packed with visitors. Fine if you wanted crowds, but hell if you didn't. And today she very definitely didn't. Some peace and quiet and solitude sounded much more appealing.

'Thanks for the offer, but I think I'll take myself off for a walk here instead,' she declined the invitation.

Jane shrugged, unperturbed by the refusal. Simon had already half offered to accompany her, and she wasn't averse to the idea. No reason why the couriers couldn't indulge in a light-hearted holiday romance of their own.

When she had left, Alison slipped on a pair of shorts in place of her jeans and thonged sandals in place of sneakers. The weather was improving daily and by the afternoons jeans were really too warm, unless practicality dictated the wearing of them. Then, sliding a book, sunglasses and some lotion

into a fabric beach-bag, she set off in the direction of
the lake, about a mile from the site's centre and likely
to be one of the most quiet areas on site today.

On the spur of the moment, she looked in at the
stables on her way. Horse-riding was one of the
activities offered at Belreynac, and now the loose-
boxes contained about half a dozen horses and ponies
of various sizes brought in from their winter grazing.
An additional attraction at the moment was a hound
bitch with a litter of puppies occupying one of the
stables. About five weeks old, their antics were
delightful to watch and Alison smiled indulgently
over the half-door as they nuzzled and butted each
other on chubby, wobbly legs.

She had been watching, engrossed, for some five
minutes when she became aware of another presence
beside her. Looking down she saw a little boy of
about seven years old trying to peer through a crack
in the door. Sympathising with his lack of height, she
found an old stool nearby and brought it across so he
could stand on it. Delighted, the child poked his head
above the door and giggled in sheer pleasure as he
watched the puppies' capers.

His laugh was infectious and Alison found herself
smiling, too. *'Ils sont très mignons, n'est-ce pas?'* he
demanded, his face lit up with fascination.

'Oui, très mignons,' Alison agreed, *'mais aussi très
coquins . . . regarde leur maman.'*

The boy giggled at the image Alison presented of
the canine mother giving her mischievious offspring
a stern glance.

A few minutes later, Alison left him to his absorp-
tion to take a look at the horses in the adjoining

stables. One had just come to nuzzle her pink cotton top with interest when she heard a door closing quietly nearby and, looking round, was just in time to see the boy, with something which suspiciously resembled a small tan and white bundle in his arms, disappearing round the corner.

In a second Alison was hurrying after him, hitching her bag over her shoulder and pausing only to re-bolt the stable door so that the rest of the puppies should not get out.

'*Arrête!*' she called, but whether the boy heard or not, he continued to run towards the orchards behind the yard. Alison broke into a run after him and was soon gaining on his short legs, weighted down as he was by the wriggling bundle. Turning his head quickly, he must have ralised that capture was not far off and made a hasty decision to relinquish his booty rather than receive a reprimand. Swooping down, he deposited the puppy on the ground and ran off as quickly as his young legs would carry him.

Alison knew she could still have caught him easily, but her immediate concern was for the puppy. It had scrambled to its feet and wobbled, not in the direction of the orchards, but towards the gate which led into the private walled gardens of the château. With a careless wriggle, it eased its small, plump body between the wooden bars and disappeared.

Alison hesitated by the gate. The big sign on it said 'Private' very clearly in four different languages. There was no mistaking the message that uninvited guests were not welcome. But this was an emergency. By the time she'd located someone authorised to enter, the puppy could have dis-

appeared for good. Quickly she scrambled over the
gate, fervently hoping the puppy would be found
and both of them out of there before anyone noticed.

There was no sign of it on the wide expanse of
grassy lawn, and she guessed it had taken refuge in
one of the flowerbeds or shrubberies adjacent to the
wall. Dropping to her hands and knees, she clicked
her tongue in what she hoped would be an appealing
tone to the puppy.

Concentrating intently, Alison did not see the
figure striding across the lawn towards her, and only
when a shadow fell across her face and a male voice
demanded brusquely, 'Do you realise these grounds
are . . .?' did she swing round on her haunches to
look up into the very face she would least have
wished to see at that moment.

'Oh! It's you again.'

Alison couldn't quite decide whether the tone
suggested anger or resigned acceptance that if
anyone was causing him inconvenience it was likely
to be her.

'If you're praying to Mecca, you're facing the
wrong way,' he advised drily.

'What . . . er . . . oh!' Alison muttered, just catching
his meaning as she scrambled to her feet. Very droll!
He was wearing dark sunglasses which hid his eyes
from view, while she had the disadvantage of having
the sun's glare directly in hers. Should she casually
remove her sunglasses from her bag and put them
on? One look at his expectant features denied the
possibility.

'Not another low-flying bat swooping down at
you?' he queried sardonically, indicating the crouch-

ing position he'd found her in.

Alison saw the funny side of it herself and was almost tempted to laugh, but she resisted the impulse. She didn't want to find this man amusing.

'No, a puppy . . .'

'Not flying puppies now?' One dark brow lifted mockingly.

'Don't be ridiculous,' Alison snapped without thinking, and immediately could have bitten her tongue off. Hadn't she brought enough trouble and worry on herself already through her exchanges with this man, without heaping more coals on the fire? She took a deep breath to calm her temper and then continued, 'A little boy took one of the puppies from the stable yard . . . when I ran after him he dropped it . . . and it came in here.' All the time she spoke, her eyes were raking the ground, desperate to find the evidence that would substantiate her story.

Glancing back up at him, she couldn't see his eyes, but his facial expression indicated some doubt as to whether he had a genuine animal lover or a complete nutcase on his hands.

Determined to prove it wasn't the latter, Alison dropped to her knees again and made a soft crooning sound. The next moment, he was down on his haunches beside her. 'You're sure it came in here?'

She nodded quickly. 'Yes, and it wasn't on the lawn so it must have hidden in the undergrowth.'

As his hands parted the plants and shrubs, Alison decided with some relief that he must have accepted her story. Not so welcome was the abrupt awareness of his proximity. The lightweight material of his trousers rippled tautly across a muscled thigh, so close it almost touched her bare one. Consciousness of his nearness tingled along her senses, distracting and irritating simultaneously. Surreptitiously she edged slightly away from him. She hadn't wanted to be amused by him. Much less did she want to be made aware of him. Not in *that* way.

Just as she was beginning to think the puppy must have disappeared from the face of the earth, a small squeak came from the middle of a rosebed. Oblivious to the barbed thorns which attacked her arms, Alison immediately reached in, groping towards the direction of the sound and foraging with her fingers until they encountered something small and furry. Grabbing it by the scruff of the neck, she gently pulled it out and craddled it in her arms as she stood up.

The puppy shivered and whimpered softly, only partially reassured by her stroking fingers, and the next moment she noticed vivid splashes of blood on her T-shirt. The Comte had seen them too and was immediately turning the puppy over in her arms to examine it. There was no obvious sign of injury—the blood seemed to be coming directly from its paw.

'What is it?' Alison raised concerned brown eyes to his.

His smile was briefly reassuring, his attention still focused on the pup. 'I think he's probably picked up a thorn in his pad,' and then, by way of explanation, 'their pads are very soft at this age and a thorn could easily have penetrated it. Bring him into the château and I'll have a proper look at him.'

The next minute he was taking hold of her elbow and leading her across the lawn towards a glass conservatory positioned at one end of the château. Alison had to hurry to keep up with his long strides, and the puppy nestled in closer, disliking the jostling movements.

Once through the conservatory, Alison found herself in a large office. The Comte . . . Maximilien . . . she was no longer sure how to address him even in her own mind—one thing for sure, he was no longer just *the man*—cleared a space on the desk and instructed her to set the puppy down there. 'Hold him still while I examine him,' he requested sparsely.

Alison did as she was asked, as concerned as he was for the small creature's welfare.

A brief examination revealed that he had been correct in his assumption and, although the puppy whined pitifully during the procedure, it only took a few seconds for the thorn to be extracted.

From a cabinet on the wall, the Comte drew out some antiseptic lotion and cotton-wool. 'We'll just apply some of this,' he murmured, screwing off the bottle top. Alison held the puppy firmly, at the same time talking to it softly, trying to reassure it that, despite what it might think to the contrary, they really were doing their best to help it.

Finally he stood upright, evidently satisfied with the treatment. 'I think the best thing is to get him back to his mother and we'll get the vet out later to have a look at him,' he stated, picking up the phone and dialling a number.

Alison concentrated on keeping the puppy still. He was already wagging his tail with renewed vigour and eyeing the contents of the desk with interest, as if assessing their amusement value.

Within minutes of the phone call one of the site workers appeared at the doorway. The Comte spoke to him in French, but Alison understood enough to know that he was instructing the man to return the puppy to the stables and keep an eye on it until the vet arrived. Then, closing the door on the man and departing pup, he turned and leaned back against it, swarthy and rugged against its cream background.

Alison followed his glance as it travelled down her T-shirt and realised what a mess she looked. Blood and mud stains did not complement its pink colour, and the arm she had thrust among the rose-bushes was a mass of scratches. But, more than that, she suddenly became conscious of the lengthy expanse of thigh exposed beneath her shorts. One look at the Comte's face told her he was not unaware of it either. 'I think I'd better . . .' she started, but got no further.

'Those grazes on your arm need some attention. I'll ask Madame Chessaud to make us a cup of coffee while I have a look at them,' he declared evenly, but in a tone which did not invite contradiction.

'Thank you, but . . .' Alison started to refuse, uncomfortable now that the focus of his attention had shifted from the puppy to her. It might have been intended as concern, but it made her feel strangely vulnerable, and she didn't like the feeling of being trapped.

'Besides . . .' he continued in the manner of one accustomed to getting his own way '. . . you will panic the campers if you walk through the site like that.' He indicated her soiled T-shirt. 'I'll find you a clean one and Madame Chessaud will wash that one.'

Before she could utter a further word of protest, Alison found herself being propelled towards the internal door of the office, with the Comte's hand firmly in the small of her back. It happened so quickly that she had no time to object, and, short of engaging in an unseemly struggle, there seemed no alternative but to comply with his suggestion. Besides, she had to admit to a degree of curiosity about the château. It had intrigued her from the outside, and this was probably the only opportunity she would get to see its interior. One cup of coffee couldn't do any harm, could it?

Maximilien guided her quickly across a very grand marble-floored entrance hall and along a corridor to the cloakroom leading off it. He held the door for her to enter, but this time it was Alison who blocked the opening.

'Thank you, I think I can manage on my own,' she declared coolly, at the same time holding out her hand for the antiseptic and cotton wool. His lips curled faintly at the corners, but he didn't relinquish the items.

She was right—he didn't give in easily. But neither did she.

He eyed the scratches. 'You may not be able to reach them all yourself.'

'I'm sure I'll manage,' she insisted drily. 'I'm very supple.'

'I'm sure you are,' he agreed, mouth twitching and green eyes flicking over her lazily, and she knew he wasn't just referring to her arms. A sexual undercurrent pulsed between them for a few brief seconds, invisible but tangible none the less. It

startled her, and the next moment she was grabbing
the antiseptic and cotton-wool from his fingers and
closing the door behind her.

His voice, threaded with amusement, penetrated
the thick, oak barrier. 'I'll be in the drawing-room if
you need me.'

Alison leaned back against the door and stared at
herself in the large, ornate mirror which occupied
almost the whole of the opposite wall. She looked
distinctly dishevelled—grubby, tousled and very,
very pink. Remaining still, she allowed her gaze to
wander round the rest of the room, about twice the
size of the average family bathroom and far more
sumptuous. Her eyes came back to rest on herself,
incongruous amid this cool, green splendour. What
was she doing here? How had she got herself into
this predicament?

At their first meeting she'd taken an intense dislike
to the man. Second impressions had hardly
improved the feeling and had caused untold havoc
with her peace of mind. Yet here she was, in his
house, in his cloakroom, about to share a cup of
coffee with him, and feeling what towards him? How
did she feel? Not dislike exactly, but certainly not
affability either. He was far too sure of himself, too
unsettling for that. In a way he reminded her of
Jonathon; perhaps that was why she found him so
disturbing.

Moving forward to the basin, she turned on the
taps and rinsed her face with cold water. Then, filling
the bowl, she bathed her arms and dried them before
applying the antiseptic. Finally she combed her hair,
brushing it back from her face. Apart from her

T-shirt, the mirror reflected a much improved reflection, cooler, more composed, the image she wanted to project.

As if on cue there was a knock on the door. Alison opened it tentatively, half expecting the Comte himself, but in fact it was a small, plump, elderly lady. Presumably Madame Chessaud. She held out a pale lemon blouse and smiled kindly. *'Donnez-moi votre chemisier, je vais le laver.'*

'Just a minute.' Alison took the proffered top and slipped off her own, handing it over for washing as requested. It really wasn't necessary, she could have dealt with it herself, but she didn't want to contradict Madame Chessaud's instructions.

Closing the door again, she pulled the borrowed top over her head, easing her scratched arm carefully into the sleeve opening. It was very pretty, very feminine. How did it come to be in the Comte's possession? she wondered.

Then, smoothing down some renegade strands of hair, Alison made her way out of the cloakroom and back along the corridor to the entrance hall. The Comte's voice called out from one of the rooms leading off it.

The room she entered was large with a high, ornate ceiling, elegantly yet comfortably furnished in blues and golds. A tray with coffee-pot and cups and saucers was set down on a low table in front of the sofa where the Comte was seated. Deliberately Alison seated herself in solitary splendour in the armchair set at right angles to it. While the Comte poured the coffees, she looked round the room, admiring the paintings and antique pieces displayed there. As he handed her a cup of coffee, she thanked him for the loan of the blouse. 'It's very pretty,' she concluded. If she had been expecting some indication of its ownership, she was disappointed.

The Comte looked up from spooning sugar into his cup, green eyes appraising. 'Very pretty,' he agreed, 'but, please, it is I who must thank you. The hound puppy is quite valuable. If you had not acted so quickly, we would have lost him.'

It was the first time Alison had heard him so conciliatory and it surprised her, embarrassed her almost, especially when she considered the way their last encounter had ended in the bar. She didn't want to be reminded of that and searched round wildly for a diversionary topic; anything would do.

'Has the château been in your family a long time?' she asked, taking a sip of the hot, strong liquid. It was a suitably impersonal topic but also one she was genuinely interested in.

'Nearly five hundred years. There have been Belreynacs here since the close of the fifteenth century. Of course, each generation has made changes, knocked down some parts, remodelled others, but essentially the chateau is the same.' He leaned back against the soft cushions at the back of the sofa, relaxed and at ease in this familiar setting.

'It must be wonderful to own somewhere like this . . . a part of history, passed from generation to generation.' Alison found herself becoming less self-conscious, more absorbed now by what the Comte had to say than simply the need to keep the conversation going.

He nodded. 'That's true, but also a big responsibility. The château and an estate the size of this one don't just run themselves. They cost an enormous amount to maintain and, like any investment, they need careful management.'

Settling herself back in the armchair, Alison warmed to the topic. 'Is that why you developed the camp-site?' she asked.

'That's right. My father was in his seventies when he died, five years ago. He'd never properly tackled the problems of rising overheads and decreasing income. At his age, he simply wanted to live out his life in the manner to which he had always been accustomed . . . and who can blame him? But, when he died and I inherited the estate, I knew that something drastic would have to be done if our family was to retain ownership.'

'But why a camp-site?' It didn't seem the most likely money-making scheme.

The Comte shrugged his shoulders. 'Elimination of options. Agriculture is no longer a sound proposition on its own, and besides, France is already over-producing. I could have turned the château into something like your English stately homes, but I did not want my home to be so accessible to the public. Amusement parks . . . safari parks . . . these were all alternatives, but none appealed. Camp-sites are big business now in Europe. I have to share the château's grounds with others for six months of the year, but the rest of the time it is mine to enjoy. It is a good compromise, don't you agree?'

Put like that, Alison had to agree. She hadn't really given it much thought before, simply accepting the existence of the camp-site, without fully considering the reasons for it or the alternatives to it.

'How are you enjoying life at Camp Belreynac?' Swiftly the Comte shifted the questioning, taking her by surprise.

What should she say? Everything was fine until I suddenly discovered that the strange man whom I disliked so intensely was the owner of the site. You! No, she couldn't say that. Besides, it was no longer true. She might not find his presence entirely agreeable, but he was not the tyrannical brute she had first thought him. Finally she settled for a polite, non-committal statement. 'It's a lovely site in a very beautiful setting. As for the work, it's early days yet, but I'm sure I shall enjoy it.'

Perhaps her hesitation in replying had been too obvious, or perhaps the reply itself was too prim, too coy; either way, the Comte seemed to find it amusing, his green eyes glinting disconcertingly. 'How very formal. You weren't quite so restrained in your views last time we met, I remember.'

He was reminding her of their conversation in the bar. She had hoped that could be forgotten. 'I didn't know who you were then. You should have told me,' she accused mildly.

His voice was a husky drawl, made even sexier by the French accent. 'Why, would it have made any difference?'

'Perhaps.'

'Perhaps that's why I didn't tell you.'

'It was still unfair.'

He laughed. 'Candour can make a refreshing change sometimes.'

Alison blushed, remembering just how outspoken

she'd been. 'That depends on your point of view. It's a bit like spicy food; you either love it or you hate it.' In her experience most men didn't appreciate frankness, not when it was directed against them.

He laughed again. She'd been right. He did laugh a lot in the right mood. 'I said it made a refreshing change. I don't think I'd like it as a staple diet.'

She smiled too. 'I guess you're right. Probably none of us would.' After all, he'd been pretty outspoken himself and she hadn't appreciated it one little bit.

An abrupt silence descended between them which she found unnerving. Despite the bantering tone of their exchanges, she sensed an undercurrent of something else running between them, impossible to define yet none the less perturbing. Carefully she set the coffee-cup down on the table and stood up, ostensibly to examine the paintings on the walls but in fact to escape the intensity of his gaze. She stood in front of one, carefully examining its geometric shapes to try to establish a pattern. 'It's a Picasso, isn't it?' she enquired over her shoulder.

To her horror the Comte stood up and came to stand beside her. 'No, it's a Braque . . . Georges Braque. He and Picasso developed Cubism, so their early style is similar. It's an easy error to make.'

He could have sounded derisive, mocking her mistake, but he didn't. Instead he made it seem understandable. Alison felt herself relaxing slightly, silently grateful for his thoughtfulness. And when he looked at her, his eyes were smiling. 'In fact, I have to confess, I don't like it very much myself. But it was one of my father's favourites—a personal gift from the painter—so I let it remain where it is.'

He sounded so human, showing such sensitivity to his late father's feelings, that Alison found herself smiling too, momentarily forgetting her uneasiness and instinctively turning towards him. It was a mistake. For as soon as she turned towards him, it wasn't his human warmth which hit her but his sheer physical male vibrancy. Gone were the confusing geometric shapes which had occupied her vision a few moments ago, and she was abruptly confronted by flesh and blood parabolas, all too obviously masculine in their conformation.

'Do you like modern art?'

How did he manage to sound so calm when her own heart was beating like a drum? Surely he must hear it. She tried to match his composure. 'I prefer more traditional painters.'

'So you're an old-fashioned girl?' he suggested softly.

His lips were only inches away from hers and she watched them form the words as if she were lip-reading rather than hearing them. 'Only in some things.' Why did her voice sound so husky all of a sudden?

'What things?'

Just in time she realised what was going to happen and tried to step backwards, but she wasn't quick enough. The Comte's hand shot out to hook her waist and pull her towards him and, even as she tried to twist her head away, his other hand came up to cup her chin and hold it still. She struggled against him, putting her hands up to his chest to try to push him off, but her efforts were puny against his superior strength, and despite her squirming his hold on her remained firm. OK, so she couldn't get away from him, but she'd learnt from past experience that passivity could also be an effective passion-killer. Nothing ruised a man's ego more than to get no response at all. That piece of reasoning was her second mistake.

Once she stopped struggling, her whole attention was focused on the kiss. For a few seconds she stood limply in his arms and then, without warning, she felt the traitorous beginnings of response start to flicker deep inside her, mere sparks at first but then with more urgency as desire fanned them into heat. Maximilien's kiss didn't demand a response; perhaps that was its insidious danger. His touch was neither insistent nor hurried as his mouth moved over hers in leisurely exploration, coaxing its soft contours apart to investigate its inner secrets.

The hands which had been pushing on his chest ceased their pressure and spread instead to span its muscled sinews beneath the fine fabric of his shirt, to feel its powerful rise and fall, the indomitable pounding of his heartbeat.

When he drew away from her, Alison, barely aware that she had even closed her eyes, opened them to stare up at him in consternation. There was no mistaking the expression on his face. Amused green eyes gleamed with satisfaction.

'I didn't think it was really true,' he said.

'What?' she demanded, irritated now by the smugness she saw in his features.

'That you were quite so untouchable as you professed to be. You're just a little slow to ignite, that's all.'

This time Alison took him by surprise when she pulled away from him. 'Not more amateur psychology?' she demanded crossly. 'You make me sound like a smouldering bonfire.'

Maximilien appeared to scratch his chin thoughtfully. 'Oh, I wouldn't say you were as good as that . . . but you do show promise.'

Alison wondered if there was anything cheap and vulgar in the room she could throw at him. 'You swine, you kissed me deliberately,' she accused. All that talk about candour making a refreshing change. What rubbish! All he'd been waiting for was a chance to get his own back. He was just like any other man—an ego as big as a football and twice as fragile.

He grinned. 'I've never been able to resist a challenge. Besides, you look very fetching in that outfit.' And his eyes sauntered downwards appreciatively.

Alison didn't know who she was more angry with. Herself for allowing the kiss to ever progress as far as it had, or this . . . this brute—no, she hadn't been wrong about him, he *was* a brute—for showing such blatant disregard for her feelings.

Crossing to the other side of the room, she picked up her bag and turned to face him, vexation etching every flushed feature. 'Thank you for the coffee and the loan of the blouse. As for the rest, it was interesting in a clinical sort of way, but hardly exhilarating.' And she gave an insincere smile, trying to look as detached as he had done.

He laughed out loud. 'Be careful, Miss Taylor, I may find such protestations even more challenging.'

Alison didn't know when any man had made her so angry. Not this sort of anger, the sort that made her want to hit out and kick with frustration. 'I do hope not. I think I'd find such repeated displays of brawn very boring.' She knew she was treading on thin ice here. After all, Maximilien was the owner of Belreynac—the very fact that had worried her after their encounter in the bar. But right now she didn't care. And certainly he didn't seem in the least perturbed by her outburst. In fact, judging by the expression on his face, he was finding her show of temper highly amusing. And why shouldn't he, when he'd had such a convincing demonstration of her acquiescence in other ways?

Swinging her bag over her shoulder as though she were taking a swing at his chin, Alison marched towards the door. She was aware of Maximilien following her but refused to acknowledge him, striding ahead of him across the hall floor and down the corridor towards his office.

He walked with her as far as the gate, withdrawing the heavy bolt to allow her to pass through in a slightly more civilised manner than her method of entry earlier.

'I'll make sure your T-shirt is returned to you,' he said as she passed through, his voice coolly amused by her discountenance.

'Thank you,' she returned frostily, already beginning to walk away and barely hearing the gate's bolt slide into position with shuddering force behind her.

CHAPTER FOUR

THE following week passed with astonishing speed. The mornings always started early with ice packs and papers to deliver, and between eight and nine-thirty the camp-site resembled the rush-hour period in a city centre, with heavy bikes equipped with huge plastic carrying-boxes replacing buses, cars and taxis. For an hour and a half the couriers pedalled furiously to and from the main shop in the centre to all the outlying areas of the site. It was an energetic start but a great way to waken up, Alison discovered. She loved the site at that time of day; the grass still damp with the night's dew, a light, misty haze allowing the first shafts of sunlight to probe through, a mellow silence hanging in the clean, pure air waiting to be punctuated by sounds of life. She liked the fact that each morning's green splendour promised a new beginning, a fresh start, untainted and undimmed by a tarnished yesterday.

Her visit to the château seemed to have taken place in some dim, distant past. She had seen nothing of the Comte during the intervening week, and the deluge of activities which had taken over her life gave their encounter a faintly unreal quality.

Impossible to deny that at first she'd been thrown off balance by what had happened; maddened by both his buccaneer behaviour and her failure to rebuff it. It made her feel weak and vacillating. She loved another man, for God's sake! How could she have simply melted into the arms of the first chauvinistic opportunist who happened along? But what was the point of brooding over it? She'd wasted enough mental energy on the infernal man already, worrying all the previous week that he would take her to task for her rudeness, and all for nothing. What had happened had happened, and no amount of willing it to be different would change anything. In a moment of weakness, she had lost control of her body's reponses for a few seconds. She was a flesh and blood woman, after all, and the Comte was a very attractive male—a few brief sparks of sexual attraction had flared between them. That was all. It was regrettable, but it wasn't the end of the world. She and the Comte occupied different worlds—there was no link between them as individuals, nor did she want there to be. What he'd done was galling, injuring her pride more than anything, but nothing like what Jonathon had done to her and certainly not worth losing sleep over.

Her T-shirt had been duly returned, freshly laundered and ironed, by one of the château's cleaning ladies. She had reciprocated with the borrowed blouse and that was the end of the matter. The puppy, whom she'd checked since, was as lively and mischievous as ever, unheedful of his adventure into the big, wide world. Alison decided it was a good philosophy to adopt and took her cue from him.

At ten o'clock the children's activities began. The Swallow Club was something which Summer Canvas had started four years ago as an experiment and which had proved so popular that it had become a regular feature of their holiday package. Operating every weekday morning from ten until twelve, it offered supervised activities to children from four to twelve years, and enabled mums and dads to have a couple of hours' peace and quiet, knowing that their offspring couldn't come to any harm.

Alison had agreed to take responsibility for running the club. She had a certificate in first aid, one of the prerequisites of the job, and, with three nieces and two nephews, plenty of ideas for activities and games.

A large marquee had been erected on the games field, well equipped with materials for painting, clay modelling, paper craft and such like, so that the club could still be held even in bad weather. So far that facility hadn't proved necessary. The days had been bright and sunny and Alison had been organising football, rounders and volleyball for the older children and more simple games for the younger ones.

As the week progressed, she found herself becoming more confident in dealing with the children and more familiar with them. It was fun to relax and join in the games and races with youthful enthusiam. The children enjoyed it too, cheering her efforts with exuberant noisiness. It was tiring work but very satisfying, and when twelve o'clock came she could judge the success of the morning by the reluctance of the children to depart. There were always demands for 'just one more go', 'one more game', 'one more race', and Alison laughingly had to put her foot down or she knew the 'just one mores' would continue well into the afternoon. Nevertheless it gave her great satisfaction to see the children reappearing day after day, their young faces bright and eager.

Her services were also much in demand as a babysitter. Understandably, because of the Swallow Club, children knew her better than Jane, and when parents came to collect them at lunch time they tended to ask her then. It was an arrangement that suited both of them. Alison wasn't much interested in joining the other couriers in the bar in the evenings, and was quite happy to give parents the opportunity of an evening out. Jane preferred to socialise and was more than happy to leave the babysitting activities to Alison.

Alison blew her whistle to signal a goal and, among the expected and usual grumblings of 'offside' and 'foul', went back to the sidelines to wait for the motley assortment of players to return to their positions.

A couple walking on the far side of the playing field caught her attention. It wasn't difficult to place the man—the Comte and a petite, dark-haired woman. He said something and the woman laughed prettily, putting her arm through his in a familiar, possessive manner. Alison was unprepared for the dull thud which kicked somewhere in the pit of her stomach region, and she blew the whistle to signal kick-off with excessive vigour. Common sense told her to cross to the other side of the pitch and turn her back on them, but some perverse masochism rooted her to the spot.

'Did you see that, miss?'

'Sorry.' She lowered her gaze to the disgruntled

features of a small boy.

'You're not watching, miss,' he protested solemnly.

Alison gave herself a mental shake. It wasn't like her to be distracted, and she knew how the children hated to sense adult indifference. Bending down, she gave him her full attention. 'Sorry, Daniel, something caught my eye, that's all. What's the matter?'

'It's Michael, he just kicked me for nothing . . . look . . . and I didn't do anything to him.'

Alison quickly inspected the damage. Nothing very serious, and she gave it a quick rub. 'Sit down for a few minutes and rest it if you like.' It was a deliberate ploy. None of the children could bear to be out of the game unnecessarily for even a few minutes.

Daniel shook his head. 'No, I'll manage.' His features took on a stoically brave expression, and Alison had to smile as he ran off, taking care to limp slightly for good measure.

It was unfair on the children not to concentrate, she reproached herself, and focused her eyes firmly on the pitch immediately in front of her. However, as soon as the game was started again, she couldn't resist glancing sneakily across to the other side. She had expected that the Comte and the woman would have disappeared, but to her horror they were still there, apparently watching the activities.

Fuming indignation kindled inside her. Good lord! She'd thought he was sure of himself, but she hadn't realised how sure. Cocksure! Of course she knew he had women friends . . . knew that his relationships were none of her business . . . but did he have to flaunt them quite so blatantly?

For the next ten minutes Alison might have been blinkered. She refused to allow her eyes to wander even a blade of grass beyond the perimeter of the pitch. When she did next look up the pair had gone, and it was only in her mind's eye that the laughing image of the two of them remained.

Jane was in a flap when she returned to the tent at lunch time. Two families had reported minor thefts and another couple were very annoyed that all the tyres on their car had been let down in the night.

Thefts unfortunately were not uncommon on a site this size, but it was unusual to get two occurring so close together. Deflating the tyres seemed like the handiwork of kids who probably thought it amusing to cause others inconvenience. It wasn't very likely that all three incidents were connected.

Fortunately the thefts were covered by the Summer Canvas insurance package, since there was little chance of either retrieving the goods or tracing the culprits.

'Is there anything at all we can do?' Alison asked.

Jane shook her head. 'Not a lot . . . all we can do is keep our eyes open and advise campers to be careful. We don't want to make too much of it, though, or it could spoil people's holidays.'

Alison nodded. 'Perhaps it's worth having a word with the other couriers to see if they've had any similar problems.'

Jane returned to applying make-up and pulling a comb through her long blonde hair—she was due to accompany a group of visitors on a boat trip on the

Dordogne that afternoon. 'Good idea,' she muttered, applying lipstick. 'I'm seeing Simon tonight, I'll speak to him then.'

Alison eased herself into the corner seat of the alcove, next to Matthew. She'd been persuaded to join Jane and the two men for a drink, to make up a foursome, she suspected.

There was to be a disco later and the lights had been dimmned in preparation. You had to peer into the gloom to see even a few feet away. Alison sipped her glass of wine, smiling occasionally in the direction of visitors whose faces she recognised. She wished she could adopt something of the relaxed, carefree mood that was so predominant among them. Outwardly her face was a mask of leisurely humour, but inwardly she longed to be away from the party atmosphere.

What a wet blanket I'm turning into, she reproached herself silently. She'd always been impatient of people who pined and moped after a disastrous romance, casting a mood of despondency over others as well as themselves. It had been easy to adopt such a matter-of-fact approach because, before Jonathan, she'd never had any disastrous experiences with men. Oh, there'd been boyfriends, plenty of them, but never anyone serious, never anyone who'd tugged at her heart the way Jonathon had. But now, she wasn't even sure that Jonathon was solely responsible for her mood. Perhaps that doubt should have made her feel better, a sign that she was getting over him, but it didn't. Her reaction today on seeing the Comte with that woman had

been unexpected, to say the least. Why had she felt
that sudden thud of jealousy? Because that was what
it was. Of course, he was attractive and sexy . . . in
fact he was very like Jonathon . . . and that alone was
a very good reason for not allowing herself to be
attracted to him. She couldn't really be attracted to
him, could she? No, the whole idea was ridiculous.
She didn't know him . . . she still loved Jonathon . . .
there were too many reasons why it was impossible.
Not unless disastrous love-affairs were addictive.
Perhaps she was going to end up as one of those
women fated to end up alone because they only ever
fell for men who would treat them badly. There
should be a vaccine against certain types of men, she
decided flippantly—like measles. A jab in the arm
would be infinitely preferable to the mule's kick
she'd felt in her abdomen earlier today.

She eyed Matthew over the rim of her glass. Now,
why couldn't she be attracted to him? He was what
her mother would describe as a nice boy. Kind,
thoughtful, a good sense of humour . . . not bad-
looking. But he didn't make her pulse beat one jot
faster and, when his thigh brushed against hers,
there was no jolt of sexual electricity. Alison sighed.

Allowing her eyes to wander aimlessly round the
room, they fell on another couple who didn't look the
life and soul of the party either. David and Helen. His
expression stony and thin-lipped. Hers glum and
unhappy.

Sympathising with Helen, Alison caught her eye
and beckoned that they should come and join their
group. She saw Helen touch David's sleeve and point
in their direction, but he shook his head and

remained where he was. In a rare moment of rebellion, Helen left him and came across to their table.

'Isn't David joining us?' Alison queried with mock disappointment as Matthew stood up to allow Helen to squeeze into the alcove between them.

'He's . . . er . . . got some paperwork to do,' Helen loyally made his excuses.

'Doesn't he know that all work and no play will make him a dull boy?' Alison chided jokingly. Nothing could make David duller than he already was.

Helen glanced anxiously towards him, concerned that he would interpret the amused interchange as a joke at his expense. 'He's very conscientious,' she insisted.

'So was Mussolini, but it didn't make him very popular,' Alison muttered drily.

Helen stifled a small giggle. 'You're right. I wish David could be a bit more relaxed . . . he takes everything so seriously,' she whispered furtively.

'How does he get on with the campers?' Alison asked. She'd often wondered what attracted David to this sort of job. Anyone less like the traditional jolly redcoat it was hard to imagine.

'To tell you the truth, I think they're a bit frightened of him,' Helen confided, only half jesting. 'He's a bit stilted with them . . . you know, never jokes or anything.'

Matthew wriggled his bushy eyebrows in an exaggerated fashion. 'Why do heroes wear big shoes?'

The others waited for the punch-line.

'Because of their amazing feats . . . get it? . . . *feats.*'
They all groaned simultaneously.

'Perhaps, after all, there's something to be said for a courier who doesn't *try* to be funny,' Alison muttered teasingly, as Matthew made to give her a mock cuff on the ear.

As the evening wore on, Alison began to feel she was playing gooseberry not to one couple, but two. Several glasses of wine had loosened everyone's tongues, and Matthew's jokes got sillier and sillier and Helen's giggles more and more helpless. They certainly seemed to have discovered something in common, even if it was only mutual weakness for over-the-top humour.

Simon and Jane had got to the stage of whispering sweet nothings in each other's ears, as Simon eyed Jane's decolletage with increasing interest.

Alison felt distinctly *de trop.* Not that she blamed the others. She'd made it clear that she had no romantic notions as far as Matthew was concerned, and if he and Helen hit it off, why spoil it? Helen deserved a consolation prize after landing David as her co-worker.

Nevertheless, she didn't want to sit like a prime gooseberry for the rest of the night, and when the others got up to dance, began to grope under the table for her handbag, intending to make a discreet exit.

An invisible voice sounded above her—the Comte. Why did he always catch her at a disadvantage? 'Would you like to dance?'

Sitting upright, Alison swept her eyes quickly over

him. A dark suit accentuated his broad shoulders, and a white shirt—made even whiter under the strobe lights of the disco—unbuttoned at the neck, drew attention to the tanned column of his neck. He resembled a sleek panther . . . lean, sinewy and dangerous, like all jungle beasts. Memories of the dark-haired woman curling her arm through his hardened her resolve. 'I don't . . .'

One dark brow lifted sardonically. 'Don't dance? I'll teach you.'

'I don't . . .' she started again.

'It's really very easy.'

And before she knew what was happening, his hand was on her wrist and he was leading her on to the dance-floor. It was a slow, romantic number and he unhesitatingly drew her into his arms, one hand curving the hollow of her spine, the other her shoulder, moulding her loosely to his length.

'See, you just move in time to the music.' And he began to move slowly and languorously against her.

Alison glared up at him. 'I know perfectly well how to dance, thank you. I was simply trying to refuse, *politely*.'

'And I was simply trying to insist, politely.' He mocked her English accent.

'That seems to be something you're very good at,' she muttered sullenly.

'Dancing? Thank you.' He deliberately misunderstood her.

'Insisting,' she corrected grittily.

'Only when the person I'm dealing with won't be easily persuaded.'

'Meaning me, I suppose.'

'You're not the most acquiescent woman I've come across.'

She didn't need to look at his face to know that he'd be smiling. He was enjoying this. Why shouldn't he? He'd got his own way again.

'I don't consider acquiescence a particularly desirable attribute to develop.'

A low, husky chuckle rumbled in his throat. 'Perhaps you should try it some time . . . it could be more agreeable than you think.'

Is that the line you used on the dark-haired woman? Alison wondered, prickling. She'd looked positively snake-charmed. 'I doubt it,' she challenged drily. 'Compliance becomes very boring.'

The hand on her back increased its pressure, his fingers spreading so she felt their span through the flimsy material of her dress. 'I agree, on its own it is very boring, but it makes an intriguing contrast.'

She glanced up at him, noting the dark shadow on his chin. it should have detracted from his looks, but only seemed to reinforce them. Her voice was a little huskier than before. 'That depends if you want to be intriguing.'

'Don't you?' he asked softly, silkily.

Alison tried to arch away from him, sensing too late the danger of this close contact. 'No . . .' she flung the denial at him '. . . I told you before, I just want to be left alone.'

'You looked lonely just now, sitting at the table.' His tone had become gentler, less mocking.

'I was alone, that's not the same as being lonely,' she corrected him.

'I agree, but nevertheless, you looked lonely.' He

refused to accept her amendment.

Alison moved mechanically in step with him, uncertain of how to respond, how to deflect the conversation, above all, how to escape.

'You got your T-shirt?'

'Pardon?' Oh, yes! The T-shirt. 'Yes, thank you.' Why was she being so polite when what he really deserved was a kick in the teeth?

'The puppy is fine again now.'

'I know, I went to see him.'

'. . . Thanks to your quick thinking.'

Not quite quick enough, Alison thought ruefully, recalling the events which had followed the puppy's rescue.

'Why do you cut your hair so short?'

'What?' The personal question took her by surprise.

'With hair that colour I'd have thought most women would want to wear it long.' He leaned back slightly, eyes skimming over her head.

Alison wasn't quite sure whether he was trying to disconcert her with the question or with an oblique compliment. She ignored both overtures. 'I'm not most women,' she reminded him drily. If he thought one fleeting kiss gave him instant access to her personality, he was wrong.

'No, you're not,' he agreed laconically, and then more mockingly, 'though you do run true to type in certain things.'

This time Alison arched away from him aggressively. 'Meaning?'

He laughed, a low, sexy sound. 'Don't look so belligerent. It doesn't suit you.'

'I don't behave to suit you.' He was far too clever at getting under her skin, nettling her.

Amusement flecked his eyes. 'You did last Sunday.'

So did that woman today by the look of you together, Alison wanted to retort peevishly, but just in time bit her tongue. Instead she yawned pointedly. 'Last Sunday, what about it?'

Amusement and something else glinted in his eyes now. Irritation? Alison hoped so. He deserved a taste of his own medicine.

'You're a cool little cat, aren't you?' he growled as his eyes flicked over her again, shrewdly appraising, and his hands tightened their grip.

Don't lose your advantage, Alison told herself firmly, trying to ignore the way his fingers were branding themselves against her skin and the way her pulse was clamouring under his scrutiny.

At that moment there was a tap on his shoulder and one of the barmen spoke quietly in his ear. Alison drew back, sensing an opportunity to get away, but at first his hand did not relinquish its grip. And then he was releasing her. 'Excuse me, there is a telephone call. Wait for me.' It was an instruction, not a request.

But as soon as he had disappeared into the gloom, Alison returned quickly to her table, collected her handbag, and made her way out of the building. She'd never gambled seriously in her life, but every instinct told her now to quit while she was still ahead. After the smoke-filled atmosphere inside, the night air was fresh and clear and she paused for a second to drink in the pure sweetness of it, feeling it purge her mind of the confusion of only a few minutes ago.

The pathway leading to the couriers' tents was an isolated one, not used by other campers, so when she heard footsteps behind her, Alison quickened her pace. The hand falling on her shoulder made her jump, though she had already guessed who it belonged to.

'What's the rush?' he asked softly.

'No . . . no rush. I just wanted an early night, that's all,' she clumsily defended her abrupt departure and then could have kicked herself for even feeling the need to.

'Liar,' he chuckled softly. 'You almost ran out of that bar as soon as my back was turned.'

'I did not,' she denied tartly.

A raised eyebrow betrayed disbelief, but for now he seemed willing to humour her. 'OK, so you wanted an early night. I won't detain you long. I wanted to ask you a favour.'

'A favour?' Alison repeated his words suspiciously. What sort of a favour? 'Yes?' It was an abstruse invitation to continue.

'I saw you today.'

'I saw you, too.' It came out too quickly, too abruptly, making it sound like an accusation.

'Ah!' The Comte said it slowly, elongating the sound, as if something had just clicked in his mind.

Alison wondered if she had given too much away in the swiftness of her response. His next words confirmed that she had.

'The woman I was with. She is my sister.'

Good grief, couldn't he come up with something more original than that? His sister! What did he take her for, a complete fool? And why bother to lie anyway? It wasn't her concern. Disbelief registered in every feature. 'Really?' she drawled sceptically.

The Comte grinned too, a smug, self-satisfied grin, as if her reaction had told him something he wanted to know. Alison didn't like it.

'Yes, didn't you see the family resemblance?' he quipped.

Now that she considered it, there was a faint similarity, the same dark colouring, the same good looks. 'I really didn't notice.' She feigned indifference, still not totally convinced.

'My *sister* . . .' he emphasised the relationship '. . . is accompanying her husband to Canada on a business trip, so my niece will be staying with me for the next couple of weeks, and I wondered if she could join in with your games sessions in the mornings.'

Alison was momentarily lost for words, and she wasn't altogether sure whether it was due to the realisation that the woman today really had been his sister or the unexpectedness of the totally innocent request.

'I . . . er . . . yes . . . how old is your niece?' She tried to sound efficient and professional.

'Eight, but she's an only child and doesn't spend enough time with children her own age. Your play activities will do her good. My sister was very impressed with the way you handled the children this morning. She wanted to speak to you herself, but . . .' and there was a faintly mocking tilt in his voice as he added these last words '. . . you seemed very intent on the football game, and unfortunately she had to get away.'

Alison felt her cheeks flushing. Had her behaviour that morning really been so transparent? It was obvious that the Comte interpreted it as jealousy . . . and wasn't he right, at least partially?

She cleared her throat. 'That . . . er . . . will be fine. She can start in the morning, if you like.'

'Thank you, Alison. You don't mind my calling you Alison, do you?'

When he looked at her like that, how could she mind what he called her? Her eyes swam in the dark shadows of his face, threshing against its attraction.

'No . . . er . . . of course not.' Why was her tongue so clumsy all of a sudden?

'Goodnight, then, Alison.'

'Goodnight . . .' She paused uncertainly.

'Try Max,' he suggested softly.

Max! She'd not even been able to manage the informality of Maximilien. 'Goodnight . . . Max.'

Alison dropped the words into the still night air as one mesmerised. And she stood just as transfixed when Max took a step towards her, tilting her chin and lowering his mouth to hers in a soft, teasing kiss.

'Good,' he murmured silkily.

And afterwards Alison wasn't entirely sure whether his comment referred to the kiss or to the fact that she had agreed to the favour.

CHAPTER FIVE

ALISON pretended to be asleep when Jane came in, guiltily ignoring the whispered repetition of her name. She was in fact wide awake, but in no mood to face Jane's inevitable questions. How could she give any answers when she hadn't worked them out for herself yet? And how did she go about doing that? She'd come to France for very real reasons and with very real intentions. Those intentions had been categoric. No involvement with men. It hadn't even occurred to her that such a condition would present any problems. She'd just lost the only man she'd ever loved . . . how could anyone else compete with Jonathon's place in her heart? It hadn't seemed possible . . . still didn't, she scolded herself abruptly. And yet, there was no denying her body's response every time Max was near. It took on a will, an instinct of its own. Undeniably, it . . . she . . . found him attractive.

Thoughts, ideas, possibilities, suggestions, all weaved themselves in and out of her mind so that soon it was just a jumbled mix of abstractions, incapable of any logical reasoning. Tossing and turning, Alison finally fell asleep in the early hours of the morning, no wiser than she had been four hours earlier.

Over breakfast there was no way of ignoring Jane's

questions. 'Why didn't you tell me you knew the Comte so well? What was going on last night? Why did you rush off like that? Why did he follow you?' Each question was graphically illustrated with speculative looks and raised eyebrows.

Pretending an appetite for croissants she didn't particularly feel, Alison dealt with the interrogation casually and dismissively. 'I don't know the Comte *that* well. He simply asked me to dance because he wanted to ask a favour . . .'

'Ah!' Jane's look became expectant.

'His niece is staying with him, and he wanted to ask if she could join in the children's activities in the mornings.'

Jane snorted derisively. 'Huh! That's a crafty move. I can hardly imagine the Comte as a doting uncle. Children aren't his scene. I bet he couldn't wait to hand her over to someone else to look after.'

The croissant paused on its way to Alison's mouth. She hadn't looked on Max's request in that light, and yet now Jane had suggested it, it sounded more than plausible. Perhaps all Max had seen her as was a useful babysitter. Maybe all that talk about the child needing company was merely a pretext to arouse her compassion.

Taking care not to betray her thoughts to Jane, she casually agreed, 'You're probably right, but one more child won't make much difference . . .' and changed the subject. 'Did you mention those thefts to Simon?'

Mouth full, Jane nodded. 'Mmm . . . amazingly, they've had three reported; that's positively epidemic for this early in the season. Usually no one thief is here for long enough to strike that many times. Not unless they're doing it professionally, but none of the items stolen have been very valuable. It doesn't make sense.'

At first Alison had only been half listening to what Jane was saying, her thoughts still on Max, but now she gave her her full attention. 'Shouldn't we report it to the local police?'

Jane shrugged, 'They won't do anything. It's only petty theft, after all. No, we'll have to see if it continues after this lot of holiday-makers have gone. If it still continues, that suggests someone who's permanently at the site.'

Alison nodded, approving the reasoning. 'That's a good point.' She could only hope Jane's deductions as far as Max's motives were concerned weren't quite so astute too.

Promptly at ten o'clock, Max arrived holding a small girl by the hand. Her pretty, dark features immediately reminded Alison of the woman yesterday and, of course, there was a resemblance to Max too.

Dressed in jeans and checked shirt, he looked casual and informal, but Alison deliberately concentrated her attention on the child, refusing to concede any memories of last night's kiss. Dropping down on her haunches, she introduced herself, *'Bonjour. Je m'appelle Alison et j'espère que tu vas bien t'amuser avec nous ce matin.'*

The child had solemn dark eyes fringed with long lashes. Her lips parted in an engaging smile to reveal a gap where two milk teeth had been and had not yet been replaced. 'Good morning, *mademoiselle*, my

name is Cécile and I look forward to spending the
morning with you.' She spoke in charming though
rather formal English, and Alison wondered how she
would cope with the rough and tumble of the
morning's activities. There was a doll-like fragility
about her which did not bode well for the boisterous
games which the other children enjoyed.

Before he left, Max spoke quietly to Cécile in
French. Alison was able to translate roughly,
understanding enough to know that he was telling
her to behave herself and not give Alison any trouble.
Who's he to talk? Alison thought drily.

It might have been a ploy to arouse her sympathy,
but nevertheless Max had been right when he said
Cécile needed to mix more with children her own
age. Alison found her to be shy and reticent with the
other children, nervous of their noisy, boisterous
behaviour. For the first hour or so she remained by
Alison's side, refusing to venture further than a few
feet away. Alison didn't push her, knowing that
children have to develop confidence at their own
pace. Towards the end of the morning, however,
Cécile started to relax a little, making friends with an
English girl of about the same age. The two sat at the
edge of the field making daisy chains and seeming to
have no difficulty with the language barrier. Alison
kept her eye on them, hearing snatches of conversation and smiling occasionally at the odd mixture of
French and English in their sentences.

On the whole, the morning went by quickly and,
glancing at her watch, Alison found there was only
ten minutes left before the activities finished. Much
as she had enjoyed having Cécile along to join in,

Alison couldn't help recalling Jane's words over breakfast. 'He's only looking for a babysitter.' The more she thought about it, the more convinced she became that Jane had been right and that come lunch time Max would arrive with a convenient excuse and an earnest plea for her to mind Cécile in the afternoon.

Under normal circumstances she wouldn't have objected. She liked children, enjoyed their company, but she hated the thought that Max might have deliberately conjured a little romantic interaction between them to further his own cause. What could be easier to a man as obviously experienced with women as Max was—a few soft words, a few kisses—and he had found himself a childminder for the duration of his niece's visit? It was a cynical interpretation of his behaviour, but Alison had learned that it wasn't wise to trust indiscriminately, and by the end of the session she had her refusal of Max's request, if it should come, well rehearsed in her mind.

Max might not have fitted the typical image of doting uncle, but nevertheless, as soon as Cécile saw him, she let go of Alison's hand and ran across to him. Strong arms picked the child up easily, swinging her towards him so that she could plant an adoring kiss on his cheek.

Alison was busy gathering together the balls, rackets and shuttlecocks which had been used in the morning's activities, so it was some time before she was able to wend her way over in their direction, but as she drew closer she heard Cécile, tongue suddenly released, tripping over herself to regale Maximilien with details of the morning's events while he listened attentively.

Alison had to turn away to shepherd the last group of children over to their parents and missed Cécile's next words, only hearing Max say firmly, 'In English, please, Cécile.'

When she finally joined them Cécile's small face was puckered in concentration as she strove to compose her request in English, 'Please will you join my uncle and me this afternoon, Mademoiselle Alison . . .' and then, forgetting all formality '. . . Oh! Please . . . Please . . . *venez, s'il vous plaît.*'

Alison frowned. Join them . . . where? This wasn't what she had been expecting.

Seeing her puzzled expression, Maximilien proffered an explanation. 'I was planning to take Cécile to visit the underground caverns at Padirac this afternoon and she would like you to come with us.'

The excuse she had made up now redundant, Alison had to search round in her mind for another one. Cécile's desire to include her in the outing was gratifying, but she had no intention of foisting herself on a reluctant Max for the afternoon.

With a child's intuition, Cécile sensed the refusal that was coming and pressed the appeal with innocent candour. 'Please, *mademoiselle*, please come with us.'

Alison looked up to Max, mutely requesting his intervention.

'Why don't you come with us? We'd like you to . . . *I'd* like you to.' Mouth curving in a sexy smile, he emphasised his own inclusion in extending the invitation.

Alison knew she must be mad. She'd promised herself to steer clear of men, Max in particular. Why was she even hesitating? And yet there was no denying the invitation's attraction. The chance to visit Padirac or the chance of spending some time with Max? Which appealed the most? Did it matter? After all, Cécile would make a very proper chaperon. With hardly any effort at all, the feeble arguments of her conscience were dismissed and she had accepted.

The Dordogne had to be one of the most beautiful areas in France, in the whole of Europe, Alison decided as she watched the countryside slip by from the front passenger seat of Max's car. High wooded hillsides of evergreen conifers broken by oak, ash, birch and beech alternated with sleepy green fields, speckled with daisies and filled with light brown cattle contentedly munching. And every so often, a glimpse of the Dordogne itself, sometimes gently bubbling as innocently as any village stream, other times roaring and rushing in powerful majesty.

A region so peaceful, so seemingly contented with its lot, happy simply to be left in peace rather than striving for change, for modernisation. It made you feel as if you had stumbled on a timeless pocket of existence, unimpressed by the outside world.

Madame Chessaud had packed a hamper for their lunch and, close to their destination, Max drew the car off the road so they could enjoy their picnic in peace and quiet. Cécile ate little, and with a child's impatience was soon eager to be on the move again.

Max had insisted that while Alison was in their company they must speak in English, so now Cécile's face was a mask of concentration as she sought for the right words to express her request.

'The rocks . . . shall I . . . *non* . . . can I climb them?'

Max nodded. 'Yes, but not too high.'

She smiled in quick acceptance, seemingly surprised and delighted that he had agreed at all.

Alison leaned back on one of the sun-baked rocks and watched the child's departing figure as she skipped happily across to a rocky embankment. Lazily she bit into a ripe peach, and then had to rub her chin with a wrist to stop the juice trickling down.

Max manoeuvred himself into a position where he could keep an eye on Cécile, and Alison wondered whether it was just coincidence that they were now less than three feet apart. His lengthy frame ranged across the chequered rug, an elbow crooked under his dark head.

Deliberately Alison brought her attention back to the child. 'Cécile seemed surprised that you allowed her to climb the rocks.'

Max's eyes flicked towards her quickly. 'Yes, I'm afraid her activities are somewhat restricted normally. How did you find her this morning?'

'A little shy at first, not really comfortable with the other children. But she settled in more towards the end of the session.'

'Nevertheless, she enjoyed herself.'

Alison wasn't entirely sure whether it was a statement or a question. Perhaps Max wanted reassurance that he had made the right decision in allowing Cécile to take part in the morning games. She nodded. 'Yes, I'm sure she enjoyed it . . . and of course, being an only child, she is bound to be a little shy at first.'

For a moment Max's expression darkened. 'It's not just that . . .' He paused, as if uncertain whether or not to continue and then said, a shade more roughly, 'Cécile did have a sister, but she died.' The words were taut and abrupt, betraying an inner anguish not easily revealed.

Alison gasped. 'I'm sorry, I had no idea.'

'How could you? It was a drowning accident, three years ago. Francine was only seven.'

Seeing how the memory distressed him, Alison wanted to put her hand out, to touch him, comfort him. But such a gesture would have presumed an intimacy she shouldn't . . . couldn't feel. Instead she said gently, 'That must have been a terrible loss to the family.'

Max nodded. 'Of course, it was a tragedy. She was a lovely child. But since then my sister has found it very hard to let Cécile out of her sight. It isn't natural for a child to be so protected.'

Alison's eyes strayed to the lone figure of Cécile, straddling one of the rocks and picking an assortment of the wild flowers which grew among them. 'It must be very difficult for your sister, though; having lost one child she must live in constant fear of losing the other.'

Max's eyes followed hers. 'I agree. But in a sense Cécile is paying the price of Francine's death. A parent's natural desire to protect, to safeguard, has, for her, become a gilded cage. She is not allowed to experience or discover for herself in case she comes to any harm. But that is not natural. Life consists of pain as well as pleasure. If you deliberately exclude the

threat of the first, then you will also exclude much of
the second.'

Alison lapsed into silence, reflecting on what Max
had said. Coming from a big family herself, with all
the noisy exuberance that implied, it was difficult to
imagine the solitary world of Cécile, touched by
tragedy at such a young age. And yet in some ways
so much of what he said could also relate to her. The
cage Max had referred to just now and that night in
the bar—despite her vehement rejection of it at the
time—didn't it really exist? Wasn't that what she was
doing, trying to build some sort of cage around
herself? A cage which would protect her from pain,
but which kept out so much more as well. She
couldn't wallow in the misery Jonathon had caused
for ever, and unfortunately one dose of misery didn't
immunise you against it a second time, but that was a
chance you had to take if you wanted to participate in
life and not just observe it through a glass partition.
At some point she would have to open the door,
venture out, take the risk and start living again.

'You're right,' she affirmed softly, and, when her
eyes met his, she wondered if he knew she wasn't
just referring to Cécile.

Max smiled. 'I'm glad we agree on some things.'

A few minutes later, he had gone to assist Cécile
getting down off the rocks and Alison was busy
collecting up their plates and containers to put back
in the hamper. Folding the rug, she considered what
different façades everyone presented to the outside
world, and how easy it was to accept and judge
someone at that face value without ever probing
beneath the surface to find the essence beneath.

Cécile, apparently just a shy, rather reserved child, but with a very real tragedy in her background which inhibited her youthful curiosity rather than encouraging it. Herself, trying to present an image of being cool, controlled—'untouchable', Max had called her—yet inside vulnerable and uncertain, still bruised by Jonathon's rejection. And Max, how much of him was hidden beneath the surface? Attractive, assured, a perplexing mixture of sardonic arrogance and dynamic charm. Yet also sensitive to his niece's problems in a way she wouldn't have thought possible. Astute and perceptive, how much had he seen through the screen she'd tried to erect to cover her own self-doubts? And why should he want to see behind it?

The visit to the underground caves at Padirac was an experience Alison would not have missed for anything. About three hundred feet down into the bowels of the earth lay the great grotto and underground river of Padirac. They had to descend in a series of lifts, feeling the chill increase as they dropped lower and lower, despite the warm sunshine they had left above them, and at the bottom embarked on a cruise along the subterranean river in flat-bottomed punts poled by guides in the manner of Venetian gondoliers. After almost a mile, they reached a small jetty where they disembarked and a guide took them on a tour of the waterfalls and caverns. With their stalactites and stalagmites, their eerie silences, their echoing hugeness, they made a deep impression on Alison's mind.

But the caves were not all that made an impression.

So many times in the afternoon, she found herself
instinctively reaching for Max's hand as he helped
her up steps or into and out of boats, accepting the
pressure of his arm on her waist as he steered her in
the right direction, turning to him for explanations or
to clarify something the guide had said. And every
time their flesh touched she was conscious, not only
of how safe his grip made her feel, but also of that
inexplicable sexual chemistry which existed
sometimes between two people. It frizzled along her
senses, startling her with its intensity and with the
instinctive awareness that Max felt it too.

When Max stopped the car beside the track leading to
the tent, Alison thanked him for the outing. 'Thank
you for this afternoon. I really enjoyed it.' The words
sounded so stilted, so formal, not at all the way she
wanted them to sound.

But Max took no notice of their reserve and, leaning
forward, he murmured silkily against her ear, 'Do
you really want to thank me?' softly so that the
drowsy child in the back seat should not hear.

'Pardon?'

Max chuckled. 'Don't look so shocked, Alison. I
wasn't about to make an improper suggestion,
merely to invite you out to dinner this evening.
There's nothing improper in that, is there?'

'No,' Alison began and then stopped, realising she
was unwittingly half agreeing to his invitation.

A half-agreement was quite enough for Max. He
leaned back in his seat. 'Good. That's settled. I'll pick
you up at eight o'clock.'

'I wasn't aware that I'd accepted,' Alison remontrated lightly.

'Weren't you?' Lazy green eyes swept over her flushed cheeks, gently curving lips, the swell of her breasts.

Under his scrutiny, Alison sensed the involuntary hardening of her nipples, the sudden quickening of her pulse, the rush of warmth in her loins. Whatever verbal objections she might raise were impotent against the all too eloquent responses of her body.

Too honest to attempt such a blatant lie, Alison made no effort to deny his gently mocking challenge, and at that moment sleepy yawns coming from the back seat provided a well-timed interruption. Alison dragged her eyes from Max to turn to the child. 'Bye, Cécile, I'll see you in the morning.'

Smiling, Cécile nodded happily.

'And I'll see you later,' Max reminded her, his voice heavy with implication. As if she were likely to forget! With a quick nod, Alison released the doorhandle and stepped out, pausing only to give Cécile a brief, final wave.

After a quick shower, Alison returned to the tent and sat down on the edge of her bed. Picking up a small hand-mirror, she stared at her reflection critically. Her features hadn't altered one jot in structure, but nevertheless her face looked completely different. More animated, more alive, than it had in months. Than it had since Jonathon.

Was it wrong to feel like this? Excited . . . apprehensive . . . tingling . . . all at once? Did it make her fickle . . . inconstant? She hadn't thought she'd ever feel this sort of response to a man again, certainly not so soon. Her mind warned her to be careful, restrained . . . but her body's response was based not on reason, but instinct. Trouble was, could she trust her instincts?

Her mind travelled back to the last time she'd prepared for a dinner date—with Jonathon. Only it had never got as far as dinner.

There had been no warning, no premonition that the day wouldn't be like any other. She had gone to work as usual in the morning and done some shopping in her lunch hour. Jonathon had been away at a conference for a few days, but he was due back that evening and she'd planned to cook a special meal for him. Such an occurrence was nothing new. In the six months they'd been going out, they had often spent the evening at his flat, relaxing over a meal and a bottle of wine, talking, loving, simply enjoying being together.

Egoistically—and foolishly, she realised now—Alison had thought she was special. Despite Jonathon's reputation as a womaniser, she thought she was different, that she meant more to him than any of his previous conquests. How blinkered she'd been. Friends had warned her, even past girlfriends, but she had put it all down to jealousy and refused to listen. Jonathon was ready to settle down; most importantly, he was ready to settle down with her, or so she thought.

There had been no cooling off period, no gradual let-down, so that she could have sensed what was happening and at least got out with some pride, some dignity. None of that.

As she'd shopped in the supermarket she had even

contemplated their relationship being permanent . . .
marriage. She loved Jonathon, wanted to be his wife.
She had missed him so much during the last few
days. In a moment of gay abandon and anticipation
of the evening ahead, she had thrown an extra bottle
of wine into the supermarket trolley.

The carrier bags were heavy and it had seemed
foolish to carry them back to work when Jonathon's
flat was so close to the shopping centre. Although
Jonathon wouldn't be home yet, she had her own key
and could let herself in. She'd leave the wine in the
fridge to chill, put the flowers in water, set the oven
on automatic. All these mundane thoughts had
passed through her mind as she turned the key in the
lock of the main front door but, heading up the stairs,
faint noises overhead made her pause. Burglars!
There had been repeated reports in the local papers
about a spate of thefts in this area . . . and the flat had
been empty for a few days.

But as she listened, the sound had begun to sound
less and less like ransacking thieves and more and
more like the noises and intimacies of lovers. Even
then she hadn't been suspicious. Why should she
have been? Jonathon was away. It was mounting
anger which engulfed her, anger that anyone,
probably young kids, should dare to break in and
make such liberal use of his bedroom.

When she had flung the door open wide, it was
difficult to know who was the more horrified. The
woman had dived beneath the sheet and Jonathon
had half got out of bed, at the same time trying to
wrap himself in the duvet. Alison had stood stock-
still, shocked and devastated by the scene before her.

Still shrouded in the duvet, Jonathon had hobbled in an ungainly fashion towards her. 'Alison . . . I . . .' But she hadn't waited for any excuse, explanations, lies . . . she had dumped the shopping bags at his feet and marched from the flat, fists clenched and dry-eyed.

She'd handed in her notice at work and, apart from a brief meeting with Jonathon which had ended with bitter recriminations on both sides, she'd seen nothing of him since.

Despite all her efforts to exorcise it, the scene still came back to haunt her. Not just the awfulness of finding them. But the questions. Why? Had there been others? Had he got bored with her? Consoling friends telling her he was an addicted womaniser and not worth the grief he had caused made no difference to the feelings of inadequacy and doubt which gripped her. If their relationship had ended openly and honestly it would have been hard to accept, but infinitely preferable to the damaging blow Jonathon had dealt to her self-respect and esteem.

The memory was a sobering one, as welcome as a bucket of cold water to the mood she was in right now. She could not . . . would not allow that to happen again. Max was like Jonathon in so many ways, good-looking, charming, confident . . . she must not allow herself to fall into the same trap twice. All he was offering was a dinner-date—fine. As long as he was prepared to accept that that was all she was offering in return.

Alison chose her dress for the evening with care, not wanting to appear too casual, and yet not too sophisticated either. She wanted to look feminine but not flashy. Since she had only brought four dresses which fell into the category of evening wear, the choice was relatively simple and she finally selected a short emerald-green creation with tiny straps at the shoulders which suited her colouring and complexion perfectly. Its neckline was modest, but it compensated with a deep V at the back reaching almost to her waist.

Jane arrived back at the tent just as Alison was applying make-up. She whistled appreciatively. 'Whose ball are you off to, Cinders?'

Alison wrinkled her nose in mock indignation. 'I've hardly been going round in rags all these weeks.'

'No,' Jane agreed. 'But you've hardly been dressed up to the nines, either.'

Pausing, Alison looked down at her dress. 'You don't think it's too smart?'

Jane collapsed on a chair in the corner. 'Tell me who Prince Charming is and I'll tell you if it's too smart.'

'It's . . . the Comte . . . Max.'

'Ah!' Jane's eyebrows rose at least six inches. 'It's Max now, is it?'

'He . . . we took Cécile out this afternoon and he just . . . well . . . invited me out to dinner to say thank you.'

Jane grinned. 'Like hell he did. The Comte doesn't invite women out to dinner to say thank you. He invites them because he fancies them.'

A frown flitted across Alison's features. 'Do you have to make it sound so crude?'

'What's crude about it? There's nothing wrong with fancying someone . . . I'm just jealous because it isn't me he fancies.' Jane grinned to show she was only joking.

Alison smiled too. It was impossible to be offended by Jane's forthright effervescence for long. She turned back again to the mirror to apply mascara as Jane's voice sounded behind her, more serious this time. 'Be careful though, won't you? I know the Comte's attractive, but he's hardly led a celibate life where women are concerned. I'd hate to see you hurt again.'

The words mirrored her own thoughts of only a few minutes ago so exactly that Alison could hardly denounce them outright. Nevertheless it wasn't something she wanted to talk about, not even to Jane. Getting over Jonathon and learning how to relate to men again were problems she had to deal with on her own. She'd had one unhappy experience, but she'd learned from it too, and it wasn't a mistake she intended to make again.

'Anything exciting happen here this afternoon?' She twisted the questioning, knowing Jane wouldn't press the point.

Jane gave a rueful sigh. 'Hardly exciting. Another couple have reported some items stolen and a new family who arrived yesterday say there's no barbecue at their tent. There was one, I know because I put it there, so it looks as if that may have been stolen too.'

Alison turned to look at her. 'Why would anyone steal a barbecue? It doesn't make sense.'

Jane shrugged. 'Goodness knows. It's all very strange. There've been too many incidents for them to be unconnected, and yet nothing that would suggest the work of a professional thief.'

'Will we have to involve the police?'

'I don't know. If it continues we'll have to report it to the site manager, and then he and the Comte will decide what action to take.' Jane spoke matter-of-factly.

Alison slipped a few items into a small, black evening-bag. 'I never realised there was so much involved in running a camp-site.'

'I think you'd better concentrate on running your own life for the moment.' Jane smiled mischievously.

CHAPTER SIX

THE journey to the restaurant passed smoothly. Max made no attempt at personal conversation, simply pointing out various landmarks and places of interest en route. Amid such impersonal topics, Alison found herself relaxing into dark tan upholstery and, while Max talked, observed him covertly beneath her sunglasses. Some men appeared ill at ease in evening wear, but Max looked as comfortable in the dark blue evening suit as he had in casual jeans and shirt earlier in the day. She noted the smooth lines of his body as he sat behind the steering wheel, hands firmly in control of the powerful machine, and she had to drag her eyes away every so often as something of interest was indicated.

Although she and Jane had dined at some of the local restaurants—partly to be able to pass on recommendations to visitors—they had been mainly of the cheap and cheerful, value for money variety. This one definitely did not fall into that category.

Unobtrusive from the outside, inside it had that subtle air of luxurious comfort which spelt 'expensive' in capital letters. Even the menu had no prices, seeming not to wish to introduce the crudity of finance into this cushioned environment. Sitting opposite Max, Alison studied the extensive range of dishes available, trying to evaluate their cost.

'Would you like me to translate for you?' Max offered, interpreting her hesitation as difficulty with the language.

'No, thank you,' Alison declined politely. 'I think I'll have *moules* followed by *Brochet à la Périgourdine.*'

Max chuckled. 'Forgive me if I sounded patronising. I forgot that you speak French.'

Closing the menu, Alison smiled too. 'There's nothing to forgive. I might have been glad of your help.'

A waiter materialised discreetly beside the table, unruffled and calm, eyes smiling distantly and impersonally. Max gave their order and requested a bottle of Bergerac Blanc Sec, one of the local wines.

As he disappeared, Max turned his attention back to Alison. 'What did you do before coming to Belreynac?'

Alison twisted the stem of an empty wineglass between her fingers. How much did she want to reveal? How much did she want Max to know about her background? 'I worked for an international law company,' she answered lightly. It was safe enough to admit that.

'Ah, that explains your fluency in French.'

Alison nodded. 'Yes, when I went to secretarial college I studied French, German and Italian. I was tempted to go to Brussels and work for the Common Market, but I chose to remain in England instead.' A dangerous comment, she realised as soon as it was spoken, inviting the question, so why leave England now? Deliberately she took the initiative before Max had time to pounce. 'You must have spent some time in England yourself, to speak so fluently.'

At that moment the waiter arrived with their wine, filling Max's glass first and waiting for his approval before filling Alison's. When he had gone again, Alison smiled at Max expectantly, refusing to allow him to replace her question with one of his own. He was very good at that.

'Yes, my father had great respect for the English public school system and I spent several years in school there. I'm glad I did. The French language may be beautiful, but the English language is international. It's very useful from a business point of view.'

'Very useful when you want to bark at English couriers in the dead of night.' Alison teasingly reminded him of their first meeting.

A frown flickered across Max's features, but he was prevented from speaking by the waiter arriving to serve their first courses. When all was settled, Alison picked up one of the oval shells from the dish before her. 'Did I say something wrong?' she asked.

Max shook his head. 'No, I was about to apologise for my behaviour that night. I thought you might be someone else.'

Now it was Alison's turn to frown. 'Who?' she asked, perplexed.

Max toyed with his glass, seeming to consider her question carefully before answering. Finally he said, 'You worked for a legal company. You must have come across industrial espionage.'

'Yes, but . . .' She failed to see any connection.

'Camping-sites are big business in Europe. One of the fastest growth industries and, like any other industry, subject to sabotage.'

At first Alison thought Max must be joking. Camp-sites were places people came to on holiday, far removed from the world of devious intrigue and dubious dealings other industries were subject to. But, if he was joking, Max's face remained curiously immobile. With a shock, she realised he was absolutely serious.

'But what makes you think there is some sort of . . . of sabotage going on . . . and why?' It still seemed an exaggerated and incongruous term to apply to the peaceful, rural beauty of a site like Belreynac.

Max gave a mirthless laugh. 'Oh, I agree it sounds crazy, but believe me it's absolutely true. It takes a long time for a site to build a good reputation, but only a couple of bad seasons to destroy it. Some of my competitors think it's cheaper and quicker to damage Belreynac's reputation than to improve facilities at their own sites. It started last year. Nothing catastrophic, just a large number of minor incidents intended to spoil people's holidays and make them decide not to return.'

Alison furrowed her brow. 'And you thought I had something to do with all this, that first evening we met?'

Max grinned. 'The thought did occur to me. Last year someone consistently tampered with the water supplies . . . campers don't appreciate turning on the taps for a hot shower and finding it icy cold instead. But I came to the conclusion that any serious spy would have a much better line than being swooped on by a bat,' he concluded wryly.

Remembering the incident and Max's questions, which she had found so rude and obtrusive at the time, Alison found it easier to understand now why he had reacted the way he had.

Their first-course dishes were removed and their main courses set down before them. Alison surveyed the enormous pike, cooked in walnut oil and garnished with truffles. Max had ordered one of the goose specialities the area was famous for. As they both started on their respective dishes, Alison returned to the subject of the site. 'What sort of incidents are you talking about . . . apart from the showers, I mean?'

Max shrugged. 'As I said, nothing very serious. Minor thefts, tyres and aerials damaged on cars, that sort of thing. Why, have you had any such incidents reported?' His expression immediately intensified.

Recalling the thefts they'd had reported and Jane's opinion that they were too many to be random, Alison nodded. 'Yes, quite a few thefts already, yet nothing of any real value.'

'That sounds familiar.'

'What are you going to do about it?'

'I have no intention of letting the culprit get away with it, don't worry. The site manager and a few of the senior staff know what's going on . . . they're keeping their eyes open.' He paused. 'In the meantime, I would appreciate it if you would keep this to yourself. I don't wish the campers to be alarmed, nor do I want to give him, or her, whoever it is, warning that we are suspicious.'

Alison nodded. 'And you're hopeful of catching them?'

Max chuckled, but it was not a pleasant sound, 'Hope doesn't come into it. I *intend* to catch them.'

Judging by the expression on his face, Alison had no doubt that he would, nor did she envy the culprits when Max did catch up with them.

When Max looked up again, the air of gravity had left his features and they had assumed once again that faintly mocking, sardonic air which she found so difficult to counteract. 'Enough of these problems. Tell me why you chose to leave England this time and come to France to work as a courier.' Green eyes regarded her speculatively.

Dammit! The man must have a memory like a computer. Every piece of information stored and ready to use in evidence against you. 'Personal reasons,' Alison answered succinctly.

'A man?'

The thrust of the question took Alison by surprise. 'You seem to have a habit of adding two and two and getting five,' she replied with some acerbity.

For a moment Max looked nonplussed at the English idiom, and then his face cleared as he registered its meaning. 'It's not difficult. Anyone who leaves a job they presumably enjoyed to take something as transient as courier work has to be running away from something. In a woman's case it's usually a man.'

Alison's mind floundered wildly as she considered how to deal with Max's questions without total rebuff, yet without opening too visible a shaft into herself either. Trust and confidence had to be gained, not demanded of people. She was willing to play by the rules. Why wasn't he? Perhaps it was about time she started playing by his rules.

'You seem to consider yourself something of an

expert in these matters. Have you had many women running away from you?' If he could get personal, so could she.

Max chuckled, a deep, sexy sound. 'Not running away, no.'

'How very modest of you,' Alison commented drily. 'Perhaps it's you who runs away, then. Maybe you're afraid of being trapped . . . of marriage.'

What's the matter with me? Alison demanded silently as she stared down at the remains of her pike. I sound positively brazen. He'll think I'm propositioning him. She picked up her fork and prodded among the bones on her plate.

Across the table, she could feel Max's eyes on her. 'Is that how *you* see marriage? As a trap?' His voice was smooth as velvet. Indifferent or deliberately cool? She couldn't tell.

'Isn't that how most *men* see marriage?' she countered.

'Any situation becomes a trap if you are unwillingly caught in it.'

'And I don't suppose you would allow yourself to be caught in anything unwillingly.' Why did he make her react this way? Angrily, tauntingly, defensively, all at once. What was more, why did such a reaction excite as much as irritate her? It didn't make sense.

'Unwillingly is a hard term to define; sometimes we do things not because we will them but because we can't resist them.'

His voice was low and husky, shivering along her spine like trailing fingers. It caused a bubble of warmth to burst in her loins, effusing through her whole being so she was sure its heat was flaunted blatantly in her cheeks. 'Isn't that just a play on words, an excuse to do what we shouldn't?' Her voice sounded a little shaky.

Max's mouth curved in a gently mocking smile. 'Alison, you sound so pious. What sort of things shouldn't adults do?'

He twisted everything she said in knots. But, more than that, he twisted her in knots. Her insides were entwining themselves into utter confusion. 'They . . . they shouldn't deceive . . . cheat each other.' This turmoil of emotions Max invoked, inevitably it reminded her of Jonathon and the way she had felt about him.

His expression changed slightly. There was seriousness as well as sensuality in its hard lines. 'Why don't you tell me about this man who hurt you so much?'

Alison shook her head. 'No, I don't want to talk about him.' And it was true, she didn't. Perhaps some time, but not yet.

'But you want to be sure it doesn't happen again?' Max asked gently.

In part at least, yes, she supposed that was what she wanted. Opening the cage door was one thing, but she didn't want to walk straight out of it and into the jaws of a tiger. Out of the frying pan and into the fire, as the saying went.

Max regarded her frankly. 'Alison, no relationship comes with a guarantee that it won't cause pain to either partner. Getting hurt is a chance we all have to take. But I do believe honesty is integral to a relationship. None of us should make promises in the heat of passion which we can't keep in the cold light of day.'

Alison tried to concentrate on what he was saying, but how could she when his voice was threaded with such raw sensuality, weaving its way through her so that her mind, her stomach, churned in heart-stopping pivots? She didn't want to feel like this, out of control, vulnerable. Her voice didn't even sound like her own as she tried to ease the sexual tension between them with a feeble attempt at humour. 'I can't imagine you getting carried away in the heat of passion.' As soon as the words were out, she could have bitten her tongue off. Why had she said that? It sounded like a blatant sexual invitation. Why did he made her feel like this? Like a sexually immature teenager, not the mature woman she was. She wanted to sound cool and sophisticated, not like some naïve adolescent.

Max's hand covered hers, so swiftly that she instinctively tried to retract it, but he held it fast. 'Can't you, Alison?' he challenged, his voice as silky as a panther's purr, his hand as dangerous as a tiger's claw. 'I can assure you I'm a very passionate man, but . . .' his eyes held hers steadily, 'I'm also old enough to know the difference between the passion of the night and the reality of the morning. I don't make any promises I can't keep. Do you understand?'

Holding his gaze, Alison nodded. She knew what Max was saying and respected him for it. He was telling her that he would be honest with her. He was not promising permanence, but instinctively she knew he would never betray her as Jonathon had done.

A discreet cough broke the charged silence which hung between them and, looking up, Alison saw the waiter ready to take their order for dessert.

Max's eyes flicked quickly from the waiter and back to her. 'Would you like a sweet?'

Wordlessly Alison shook her head. Her appetite had been completely satisfied and the hunger she felt now had nothing to do with food.

'Good.' Max's short response indicated his concurrence with her wish to prolong the meal no longer.

While Max dealt with the bill, Alison excused herself and visited the ladies' room. A strangely provocative image stared back at her from the large gilt mirror on its wall, every feminine feature highlighted as if by some vital, invisible force. She looked as she felt herself to be, feminine, sensual, alluring, and there could be no doubt who was responsible for her appearance: Max.

In a sense the image frightened her. It reflected a woman, essentially herself, yet in some way separate, detached. This woman's response to Max was purely sensual, based on some indiscernible yet potent sexual chemistry which exploded between them, impossible to ignore yet equally impossible to define. It was a powerful, overwhelming force, dismissive of rationality and restraint. An all too easy force to surrender to. But what about her other, inner self? The one who had been hurt and bruised by Jonathon? Was she ready simply to abandon herself to a force propelled by sexual attraction, with all the dangers that implied?

Alison closed her eyes, compelling her mind to

focus not on the external image but on her inner feelings. Was it just her body responding to Max? Instinctively she knew it wasn't. After initial dislike and antagonism, she had discovered much to like and respect in him as a man. There was depth to his character, a rare understanding of human nature, strength yet sensitivity too, all qualities she admired. No, much of her attraction pivoted on the man himself, independently of his physical appeal. But even so, did that mean she was ready to embark on an affair with him? Because that was really what their conversation had been about.

Only two months ago she'd been in love with another man, and, despite everything he'd done to her, she wasn't sure even now that she'd stopped loving him. And, if she still loved Jonathon, what exactly were her feelings for Max? Liking, admiration, sexual attraction . . . all strong feelings—perhaps even magnified by the fact that she was on the rebound from Jonathon—but not love. And a love-affair without love was not something she could contemplate.

She was frightened of being hurt again, it was true, but Max was right, no relationship carried guarantees and, if she wanted to start living again, she would have to take her chance along with the rest of the human race. But there was more to her wariness than that. There was more to affairs than simply not getting hurt by them. At least, there was to her. She'd always had strong feelings about casual sex, not sanctimonious in her attitude to other people, but always recognising that it wasn't right for her. Sex was an expression of love in a relationship, not a substitute for it, and at no time during the evening had the word love entered their conversation. How could it, when there was still so much they didn't know about each other?

What she really needed was time. Time to establish her feelings for Max, to know what his feelings were for her. But would Max be willing to give her that time?

The journey back to the site was a silent one, both seemingly preoccupied with their separate thoughts. Or were they so separate? Alison wondered. Were Max's thoughts wandering through the same mazes as hers? If they were, he hid it remarkably well. The self-possessed features of his face gave nothing away, and she could only guess at the thoughts which might be passing through his mind.

When Max drew the car to a halt on the dark, deserted roadway beside her tent, Alison fumbled clumsily on the floor for her evening-bag. Only Max's hand on her arm halted her and, without even looking at him, she knew beyond any doubt that he was going to kiss her and that she wouldn't do anything to stop it. Instinctively her face turned to his, invitingly her mouth lifted to his, and the next second her lips met his in a kiss which assaulted her senses. Her mouth, her nostrils, were filled with the taste and smell of him, while her hand came up to entwine in his hair, wanting to feel its rough texture between her fingers. Max's hand curved round her neck, drawing her closer and then cursing under his breath at the restrictions their positions imposed.

Gently pushing her away from him, he traced the

contours of her lips with his thumb. 'This place is a little too public for lovemaking.' Huskily he reminded her of their lack of privacy in this public area.

Mutely Alison nodded, at the same time running her tongue over her lips in an effort to lubricate them. Max's kiss had drugged her senses, leaving her bemused and dazed. 'Yes, you're . . . you're right. I . . .' What could she say? I wasn't thinking? She hadn't been thinking at all. Not of their exposed position, and certainly not of what inference Max would draw from her willing response.

A finger caressed her cheek, dragging her gaze back to his. 'That isn't to say we can't go somewhere more private.'

Abruptly Alison felt ashamed of her behaviour. In the restaurant, here just now, she'd given Max every reason to believe that she wanted, indeed was eager for, their relationship to progress from friendship to intimacy. But in fact she wasn't at all sure that was what she wanted.

'But you would perfer not to.'

Max's voice cut into her thoughts. Not angry, as she might have expected, but quietly perceptive.

'You . . . you don't mind?'

A husky, mocking denial sounded in Max's throat. 'What were you expecting? That I would drag you off to the château by your hair?' Then, more gently, 'Ten years ago, yes, I would have minded very much, but that is another advantage of getting older: you learn patience. You come to realise some things are worth waiting for.'

The throaty inflection and heady implication of his

words sent an involuntary quiver of sensual pleasure down Alison's spine. Physically her body ached for him, but emotionally too her heart reached out to him. He wasn't trying to push her, use his sexual charisma to satisfy merely physical desire. He wanted more than that and he was willing to wait until she was ready too.

'And now,' he gave her chin a gentle tug, 'I think you'd better go before my caveman impulses get the better of me.'

Wordlessly Alison nodded, reaching down for her handbag and releasing the door-catch simultaneously. 'Thank you . . . for everything,' she murmured, sliding backwards, and she knew he would understand exactly what she meant.

Thrusting the car into gear, Max progressed slowly along the roadway. He didn't feel like driving slowly as the camp signs instructed, he would have preferred to push the car and himself to the limits of its speed and his endurance. Years ago, when his sexual demands were dependent on frequency rather than discernment, he had discovered that the stimulation of intense speed could provide a passable substitute for sex, if sex was all you wanted. But essentially he knew that speed would not provide any substitute tonight.

It would not have been difficult to overcome Alison's hesitancy. Her response to his kiss had told him that. But experience had taught him that lovemaking fringed with doubts and uncertainties was rarely satisfying to either partner. At the moment she was still smarting from some past experience with a man. But that pain was fading. For the time being he could wait.

CHAPTER SEVEN

THE next two weeks passed in a delightful haze of sunny days engaged in courier work and golden evenings spent with Max. Cécile continued to join in the games sessions in the mornings, gaining in confidence and enthusiasm as the days progressed. Sometimes she spent the afternoon with Alison; sometimes the three of them, Cécile, Max and Alison, spent the afternoon together. It was an idyllic period, and Alison couldn't remember when she had last felt so happy or so relaxed. Life was good. She tried not to think too much of the future, or the past, disciplining herself to savour the present. Her liking, respect . . . and attraction for Max grew daily. She observed him at work as the decisive, confident owner of Belreynac, at play as the affectionate, fun-loving uncle of Cécile, and finally as a lover. For, although they were not lovers in deed, every whispered endearment, every caressing touch, every passionate kiss, strengthened her desire for him, leaving her at night with an aching emptiness inside which only Max could fill.

True to his word, he had made no further attempts to push their relationship into intimacy. But Alison was intelligent enough to know that Max was not a man who would wait indefinitely, and woman enough to know that she could not expect him to.

On the Friday evening of the second week, Alison had agreed to babysit for the Davisons' young daughter, Kim. It was Kim who had befriended Cécile on her first morning at the activity sessions, and the two had become inseparable friends. Max hadn't been entirely pleased when she told him of the engagement, but he accepted that she had obligations associated with her job which had to be fulfilled prior to personal ones. Besides, he had some paperwork to deal with which would keep him occupied.

After reading Kim a story and tucking her up in bed, Alison settled down in the tent's main living area. She'd come equipped with writing paper and envelopes, determined to spend the evening profitably by catching up on letters to her family. She'd just finished a long, newsy one to her parents when a noise came from the other side of the doorflap. Alison glanced at her watch. Nine-thirty p.m., too early for the Davisons to have returned.

Getting up to investigate, she peered through the opaque plastic window and quickly released the door-flap as she recognised Jane and Simon outside.

'We didn't frighten you, did we?' Jane asked belatedly. 'We didn't want to call out in case we woke Kim.' In fact Jane didn't look in the least bit worried about either possibility. The expression on her face could best be described as one of suppressed excitement, and Alison wondered what could be the cause of her flushed cheeks and bright eyes. She could hardly contain herself. 'Alison, you've got to get down to the bar straight away, there's . . . there's a telephone call for you.'

Jane's voice sounded very odd indeed.

'A telephone call! Who from?' Alison asked, perplexed. Who on earth could be phoning her here at Belreynac? 'It's not my parents, is it?' she asked hurriedly, thoughts of a family accident or problems beginning to run through her mind.

Jane's face was a picture of feline secrecy. 'I can't tell you . . . go and find out for yourself.'

Alison frowned. 'Look, if this is some sort of joke . . .'

'No joke, honestly. Just go and see,' Jane beseeched.

Alison looked from one to the other. Simon stared at the ground sheepishly. Did April Fool's Day fall at a different time in France? Was she the victim of a hoax? Whatever the explanation, she had to admit Jane had aroused her curiosity. 'But I'm babysitting. I can't leave Kim,' she pointed out.

But Jane was already shooing her towards the door, 'We'll stay here until you get back,' she insisted firmly.

Slightly apprehensive, and still not altogether sure that this wasn't a prank orchestrated by Jane and the other couriers, Alison set off towards the bar. Undeniably intrigued, her mind swept over a range of possibilities and just as quickly dismissed most of them.

She paused at the entrance, peering though the dimly lit room. The telephones were situated on the other side of the bar counter and she had to wend her way through the assorted groups of drinkers, talkers and dancers to get to them. Ducking and twisting, she got to within sight of them, but both receivers were in position on their cradles. If it was a phone call from England, perhaps they'd got fed up with waiting. Would they phone back? If it was her parents, surely they wouldn't leave her in suspense? Alternatively, perhaps she should ring them just to check everything was OK.

As Alison debated whether to phone straight away or wait for a few minutes, a voice sounded behind her, achingly familiar. 'Hi, sweetheart.'

Numbly, as if on automatic pilot, she turned round to face the very last person she had expected to see.

He smiled, that smile she knew so well, sensuously intimate. It had lost none of its charm. Dark blond hair just curled on the collar of his velvet jacket, blue eyes crinkled.

'Hello, Ali,' he greeted her with the familiar nickname, just as if there had been no disagreement, no estrangement between them.

'Hello, Jonathon,' she observed smoothly, as if finding him here was the most natural event in the world, though in fact her pulse was clamouring wildly and she felt her mouth go dry with nervous apprehension.

Jonathon took her hand and quickly pulled her down to sit in an empty alcove, easing himself in beside her, so close that she could feel the heat of his thigh as it pressed against hers.

This must be a dream. How could Jonathon be here, materialising out of the blue like a mirage in a desert? And why was she calmly sitting here beside him, as if nothing had ever happened between them?

Jonathon pressed a glass of whisky into her hand. 'Here, drink this. You look as if you've seen a ghost.'

She felt as if she had, too. Whisky wasn't her

usual drink, but she took a gulp of the amber liquid, feeling it scorch the back of her throat, making her choke, Jonathon's hand came up to pat her back and then remained there, hung loosely round her shoulders.

Alison gripped the glass tightly between her fingers, needing to feel the reassurance of its hard, smooth surface, needing to be convinced that all this was actually real. That Jonathon's hand, his thigh, the smell of his aftershave, were all real. Could the mind conjure such sensory delusions?

Jonathon's hand came up to fondle the strands of red-gold hair between his fingers. 'You cut your hair,' he said, making it sound like an accusation.

'Yes, I . . . I fancied a change,' Alison murmured. What was she doing? What was she saying? Sitting here making small talk with this man who had hurt her so much. Tell him, tell him, she demanded of herself. Tell him you cut your hair because you wanted to destroy everything in your life he had touched. But of course she didn't say anything of the sort. Instead she took another gulp of liquid, feeling its raw heat slide down her throat, dulling her senses.

'What . . . what are you doing here?' she asked at last. It still seemed incredible that the images of Jonathon she had carried in her mind, of him in the office, at home in his flat, in the pub, should suddenly all have materialised in the flesh, here at Belreynac. The very last place on earth she would have expected to see him.

He laughed, a low, sexy sound. 'What do you think I'm doing here, baby? I've come for you.'

At that moment a shadow fell across the table and,

looking up, Alison saw Jane, her face a stark contrast
to the one she'd presented half an hour ago. Instead
of clandestine excitement, her expression registered
pale anxiety. Her glance travelled quickly from one to
the other and then settled on Alison. 'You'd better
come back to the tent straight away. It's Kim. She's
disappeared.'

In a second Alison was pushing against the table
and getting to her feet. 'What do you mean,
disappeared?'

'Just that . . . I found the flap to her sleeping
compartment open and when I went in to have a
look, she wasn't there.' Jane's voice was tightly
apprehensive.

Questions sizzled in Alison's brain. How could
Kim have disappeared from the tent without Jane and
Simon noticing? It just wasn't possible. 'She must
have hidden somewhere.'

Jane's hands twisted together in a nervous gesture,
'No, Simon and I have searched everywhere inside
the tent. There aren't many places she could have
hidden. She's just not there. I've left him searching
outside now.'

Even Jonathon seemed to register the urgency of
the situation. As Jane's staccato sentences finished,
he was taking Alison's elbow and leading her
towards the doorway.

The three of them hurried along the road which led
to the area where the Davisons' tent was situated.
Again Alison asked Jane to recount exactly what had
happened. There wasn't much to tell. Jane and
Simon hadn't heard or seen anything odd until
they'd actually found the child missing. Alison's

mind worked furiously. How could a small child have disappeared from a tent in full view of two adults? It wasn't possible. Could a kidnapper somehow have got in from the back? The person who'd been responsible for the thefts and other damage, had he or she changed tactics and decided to orchestrate some more drastic incident? The awful possibility occurred to her. No. she was being melodramatic. There would have been signs of a struggle, some clues. Determinedly she thrust the suggestion away. She mustn't panic, must stay calm. There had to be some simple answer.

As soon as they arrived at the tent, they encountered Simon outside. 'I've looked round everywhere . . . she's not here.'

Alison tried to resist a mounting fear. 'Perhaps she's frightened . . . she doesn't know you too well. Let me try.'

Calling softly so as not to disturb the other campers, Alison circled the tent, repeating Kim's name. Please, please respond, she begged silently.

'Kim, it's all right. If you're hiding, just come out. No one's going to be angry with you, darling.' For nearly ten minutes she repeated the reassuring phrases, but it was useless. There was no reply, no sound at all.

The full realisation of what was happening hit Alison. A child was missing. A child who had been left in her care. What on earth could have happened to her? The possibilities were almost too horrendous to contemplate. And it was all her fault. She should never have left her. Panic and guilt exploded simultaneously. She tried desperately to think straight and turned to the others who all seemed to be waiting for her to suggest the next step. 'It's no good. We're going to have to alert someone else. A proper search will have to be organised and the parents notified. Simon, you go and find the site manager. I'm sure the light was on in his office when we passed. With any luck he'll still be there. Jane, you go and ask at the other tents to see if anyone heard a child crying or any other unusual noise. Try not to alarm them. We'll stay here in case Kim comes back. She knows me best and won't be frightened to return if I'm here.' That's if she can return on her own, she thought silently.

It felt better to be doing something positive, but nevertheless, with Jane and Simon dispatched, Alison felt the full burden of guilt bearing down heavily on her. Her shoulders slumped and tears threatened. If anything had happened to the child, she would never forgive herself. When Jonathon's arm went round her shoulders in a gesture of support, she accepted it gratefully, desperately needing the warmth of another human being to combat the terrifying chill that was creeping through her veins.

It seemed an age but must in fact only have been about ten minutes before Simon returned. The manager's short, plump shape swung breathlessly into view beside him, and a third, taller, more powerful frame than either of theirs accompanied them. Max! Alison hadn't expected to see him and was amazed at the surge of relief which flooded through her as he appeared. Thank God, Max would know what to do.

She'd almost forgotten Jonathon's arm round her

shoulders, and it wasn't until the expression on Max's face tightened perceptibly at the sight of them together that she remembered it. He stood, less than three feet away from her, darkly silhouetted against the night sky, reminding her strangely of the first night they'd met and suddenly seeming just as distant and remote.

Almost simultaneously Jane rounded the corner of the neighbouring tent, accompanied by its occupant, a middle-aged woman in curlers and dressing-gown, her plump figure stiffly erect as her voice rose up shrill and accusing in the cool stillness of the night air. 'I'm not surprised the child's gone missing. It's a wonder those two noticed at all, the noise they were making.'

Alison glanced quickly from the woman to Jane, whose face flushed guiltily.

'What do you mean?' Max demanded curtly.

The woman's lips thinned disapprovingly. 'Shocking, that's what I call it. My husband and I could hear the racket from our tent . . . giggling and making God knows what noise . . .' She sniffed in disgust. 'Call themselves babysitters. It's obvious what those two were interested in and it wasn't babysitting.'

Max's hard glance swept over the small group. 'Who was babysitting here?'

Alison swallowed hard. 'I was . . . but . . .'

Max gave her no opportunity to continue, though his look scorched her. 'Spare me the buts. What happened?'

Jane seemed to recover her wits first. 'It's the child, Kim. She's just disappeared. We've searched round

the tent and called her name but there's no sign of
her.'

In an instant Max had assessed the situation and
taken control. 'Alain,' he addressed the site manager
and spoke a few words rapidly in French, telling him
to get men together with torches and start a search
party, concentrating on the area within a half-mile
radius of the Davisons' tent. Before Alain left, Max
turned back to Alison, his expression cold and utterly
devoid of any human warmth. 'Do you know which
restaurant the parents have gone to?

She nodded bleakly. 'La Fontaine.'

Max instructed Alain to get a message through to
them, asking them to return to the site immediately.

He muttered a few words privately to Alain, and
when the site manager had left Alison approached
him, venturing quietly, 'What about us? What can we
do?'

Max's mouth curled distastefully. 'Don't you think
you've done enough damage for one night?' he
demanded coldly, then, as he smelt the whisky
fumes on her breath, 'And you've been drinking.
What the hell did you think you were playing at?'

Alison faltered under the sheer venom of his glare.
She couldn't deny she'd been drinking, but she
wasn't drunk. And none of what Max was thinking
about her was true. 'Please, Max, you've got it
wrong.' She spoke quietly so the others wouldn't
hear, trying to reach the Max she knew, not this icy,
aloof stranger. But the steely hardness of his eyes and
the rock-like severity of his features told her all too
eloquently that he was beyond her reach. Faced with
such deliberate rejection, Alison abandoned all

attempts at an explanation. That wasn't important right now. All that mattered was that a child was missing and that they had to do everything possible to find her. 'Please, we want to help,' she pleaded softly.

The look Max slanted them all was frankly distasteful, but common sense must have reasoned that all assistance would be helpful. 'You,' he indicated Jane, Simon and Jonathon, 'you go down to the main complex and search there. The child knows her way down there. It's just possible she went off looking for her parents . . . since no one here seemed to be looking after her,' he added, the words cutting through Alison like cold steel.

'You,' he glared at Alison, 'come with me. The child knows you. She's more likely to come if you call than if I do,' he added by way of explanation, making it clear that her company was a matter of expediency and not personal preference.

'We'll try the woods,' he instructed. 'She could have walked that far.'

Stumbling behind him, Alison ventured an explanation, 'Max, you don't understand . . .' She got no further. He swung round, his face a mask of studied indifference. 'On the contrary, Alison, I understand perfectly well.' The finality in his voice made it clear that that was the end of the conversation as far as he was concerned.

Alison swallowed hard. 'Please, Max, let me explain. I wasn't . . .'

A cracking twig made her jump, and Max put his fingers to his lips in an impatient, silencing gesture. They both stopped dead in their tracks, silently watchful, waiting to see if the sound would be repeated. It wasn't. Max indicated that she should call out Kim's name. Alison ran her tongue over dry lips in an effort to lubricate their immobility and called out softly. No response. She called out again. Still nothing.

Max shook his head. 'Probably a fox,' he murmured, turning back to head along the path. Alison followed silently. In a sense Max was right. What did explanations matter now? They could come later. Right now a child was missing and indirectly it was her fault. She should never have left her. If she'd stayed, this would never have happened. The recriminations formed a dull, thudding chant in her brain, deadening all awareness except that of her own culpability.

Around them the wood was silent and eerie. Trees, attractive and graceful in daylight, stooped in watchful, sinister shapes in the darkness. Surely Kim would never have wandered into here on her own? It would be frightening, repellent to a child. And if she hadn't wandered off on her own, had someone taken her? Alison wanted to scream, to deny the possibility. Please, please, don't let anything happen to her, she silently begged.

Max's search was painstaking and thorough, pausing every few seconds to prod among the undergrowth and call out Kim's name, but it produced no child. Eventually the woods cleared and, only yards away, the surface of the lake could be seen shimmering like the surface of a mirror in the moonlight.

The lake! Alison hadn't thought of that danger.

Surely it was too far away for the child to have walked? It had to be.

One look at Max's face and she knew exactly what awful possibilities were going through his mind. Three years ago his niece, Cécile's sister, had been drowned. What terrible memories must this scene be reviving? Alison longed to put her arms around him, to comfort, reassure him in some way. But his expression, the taut bearing of his frame, told her all too clearly that the liberal intimacies of the last week were no longer her right. Why wouldn't he listen, let her explain? Later, later, when Kim had been found safely, as she surely must, then she would explain. But what exactly would she explain? For out of the blue, totally unexpectedly, Jonathon had appeared. *For her.* That was what he'd said, and how was she going to explain that to Max?

But, right now, all that mattered was Kim. What did it matter where responsibility for her disappearance lay? The point was, she was missing and she had to be found.

Gently Alison tried to calm what she knew must be Max's fears about the lake. 'I don't think Kim would have come this far. She's only small and, at night, these woods would seem terrifying to her. I think you were right about her heading for the centre, somewhere she knows . . .' Her voice trailed off. Was she just muttering useless, empty platitudes, trying to reassure herself as much as Max?

He shook his head, more, she sensed, to shake away the frightening possibilities this scene conjured than to deny her suggestion. Beside him, Alison shivered. She'd forgotten to bring her jacket with her and now the night mist settled on her bare arms, cold and foreboding. Without saying a word, Max shrugged off his own jacket and handed it to her. 'No, really,' she tried to refuse.

'You've caused enough trouble already. Don't make it worse by catching pneumonia.' There was no concern in his tone, only brute indifference. With rough, jerky movements Alison pulled the jacket round her. Damn him! Damn him! And damn her for caring so much what he thought.

Silently they returned to the camping area. With their own hopes of finding Kim gone, they could only hope that one of the other groups might have located her. But there was no such relief. All the other searchers had drawn blanks too. Alison's hopes of finding the child safe plummeted as one by one they shook their heads.

The Davisons had returned by now and Max spent a few moments talking to them alone. Alison heard Mrs Davison's anguished sobs and wanted to cry too. She felt as if she was being rent apart.

When Max came out, he beckoned Alison to him. 'We're going to have to call in the police. You'd better come down to the office with me so you can give them a full description of what she was wearing. You were the last one to see her.'

Alison nodded mutely.

Walking silently down towards the main complex, Alison thought about what all this would mean to Max. Once the police were called in, the media wouldn't be far behind . . . and what of Belreynac's reputation then? Whoever the troublemaker was, he or she would be rubbing his or her hands in glee. 'I'm so sorry about all this, Max.' Feeble, inadequate words, spoken more to herself than to him.

Max didn't even look at her. 'So am I,' he murmured coldly.

They'd just reached the T-junction where the paths diverged, one leading to the centre, one to the children's playing area, when a faint hope occurred to Alison. What was it she'd said earlier about Kim going somewhere she knew? 'The children's play area . . . Kim knows her way there,' she blurted the possibility out loud.

Max didn't wait for further reasoning. He nodded quickly, 'OK, it's worth a chance,' and broke into a run. Breathlessly Alison followed behind.

They scoured the play area but there was no sign of Kim. After the brief spurt of optimism, Alison felt her hopes begin to diminish again, then she pointed towards the marquee. 'Let's look in there.'

Inside the huge canvas area, Max flashed the torchlight from left to right and finally the beam picked out a small patch of pink material.

Alison pushed her way between the tables and chairs, and there, curled up tight in a corner, fast asleep, lay Kim. Alison knew she had never experienced such relief before. It swept over her in all-encompassing waves, and the next second she was on the ground, lifting the slumbering child towards her and cradling her in her arms. Sobs rose in her throat and tears began to trickle down her cheeks.

Max reached down too and some of the harshness left his expression as he gently stroked Kim's fair hair. He paused for a few moments, allowing Alison to release the pent-up emotions of the last two hours, before swinging the child up into his arms.

CHAPTER EIGHT

INEVITABLY, Alison slept badly. Despite the fact that Kim had been found safe and well, nightmarish visions of other possibilities constantly surfaced, making her toss and turn uncomfortably. Waking suddenly, she would momentarily experience the vivid conviction that the nightmares were true, before consciousness brought its own reprieve and she would sink back once more into fitful sleep.

After Kim had been found, the tensions of the evening evaporated like mist in the sun as far as the other searchers were concerned. All was relief and thankfulness, and they had drifted off, chattering volubly among themselves about an experience that would no doubt be a topic of conversation on the site for weeks to come. Max had taken the child in to the parents alone and, accepting that this was neither the time nor the place for explanations or apologies, Alison and the others had returned to their tents.

Simon and Matthew had offered to do Jane's and Alison's chores in the morning so they wouldn't have to worry about the usual morning jobs and, since it was a Saturday, there was no Swallow Club to organise. Jonathon, either due to his own tiredness or concern for her—Alison wasn't exactly sure which—had ended the evening with an undemanding kiss on the cheek and an agreement that they would meet for lunch the following day in order to 'talk'.

Once alone inside the tent, Jane had sheepishly volunteered an apologetic explanation of what exactly had happened in the earlier part of the evening. Apparently Jonathon had approached her in the bar, asking if she knew Alison's whereabouts. Jane had been almost as surprised as Alison to see him, and when he suggested the ploy of using a fake telephone call as a way of bringing Alison down to the bar, had readily agreed. 'It seemed wildly romantic at the time,' she pointed out feebly. 'After all, he has come over five hundred miles to see you.'

Alison sighed. She could well imagine the poetic image Jonathon had presented of himself and his powers of persuasion. That wasn't that she blamed Jane for. It was Kim's disappearance.

Finding Kim gone had genuinely shocked and horrified Jane. Apparently she and Simon had been 'messing around', as she coyly put it, kissing and giggling, and hadn't even heard Kim stirring. Jane admitted herself that their behaviour had been patently irresponsible and Alison knew she meant it. Further recriminations from her would achieve nothing.

Kim herself had been too sleepy to volunteer any kind of explanation for her actions, but Alison could only assume that the following day would bring its own clarification of what had happened and a confirmation of Jane's story. The knowledge that Max would be made aware of the truth of the situation brought some comfort, but it was insignificant compared to the degree of guilt Alison still felt for having left Kim at all and the new shock to her senses of Jonathon's appearance.

When daylight began to penetrate the canvas, Alison gave up any pretence at trying to sleep and peered squint-eyed at her watch. Six o'clock. Her body felt drugged and sluggish, her mind heavy. She couldn't lie here any longer, racked with guilt and worries. There was only one way to calm her mind at this unearthly hour. A swim. Occasionally on other days when she had woken up particularly early she had visited the pool. It was invariably deserted at this time of the morning and she'd been able to swim length after length without the impediment of other swimmers, feeling her body respond to the physical demands, her mind concentrate totally on the exercise. It was like a form of meditation, calming and relaxing.

Creeping about quietly so as not to waken Jane, Alison slipped on a one-piece blue bathing costume and picked up a multicoloured towel, pushing her feet into thonged leather sandals.

As expected, the pool was deserted, water lapping invitingly against the sides. The water was always cool at this time of the morning; being solar-heated, it didn't start to properly heat up until midday, in readiness for the busy afternoon period when it was most in use.

Alison didn't hover on the edge. She found the slow method of putting in a toe, then a foot, far more agonising than the quick shock of total immersion. So, having removed her sandals and thrown her towel over a chair, she performed a graceful dive into the water and started swimming systematically from one end of the pool to the other. Her arms curved gracefully, cutting the water with neat, even strokes. After about twenty lengths she stopped, levered herself out and sat on the edge, allowing her feet to gently paddle the water.

Sounds of footsteps heralded the approach of someone else and Alison looked up in some surprise to see who the other early riser could be. Her expression froze as Max rounded the corner.

Any other morning during the last week she might have made a joke along the lines of 'great minds think alike', but this morning she was in no mood for clichés and, judging by the formidable expression on Max's face when he caught sight of her, neither was he. He was wearing black swimming shorts with a towel hung loosely round his neck. She had never seen so much of him exposed before, such explicit evidence of the raw masculinity which emanated from him, and it took some effort of will to hold his gaze and not shy away in shameful recognition of the way he could affect her, despite everything that had happened last night.

His footsteps slowed slightly when he caught sight of her, but didn't stop until he was right beside her, glowering down from what seemed a great height.

'Sampling the delights of Belreynac, Alison? Make the most of it. This'll be the last opportunity you get.'

'What do you mean?' she demanded, frowning.

He laughed, a harsh, humourless sound. 'If you imagine I'd allow a courier, any courier, who becomes so engrossed in her lover that she causes a child to become lost to remain on my site a day longer, you're mistaken.'

Alison wasn't sure which angered her most. His insolent use of the word 'lover', or blaming her exclusively for Kim's disappearance. On both counts he was wrong.

'Jonathon is not my *lover*,' she retorted, scrambling to her feet.

Max's mouth curled in a laconic smile, but his eyes remained cold as glass. 'Boyfriend, then. Why argue over the term when we both know exactly what your relationship is?'

'He's neither my boyfriend nor my lover,' Alison contradicted tartly. She didn't know exactly what definition her relationship with Jonathon came under now, but it certainly did not fall into either of Max's convenience categories.

Max ran his fingers through his hair in an impatient gesture. 'Lover . . . boyfriend . . . I don't give a damn which term you use or what you do with him. What I do care about is this site, and when your behaviour endangers other people's lives then I want you off it.'

How dared he threaten her with dismissal? 'You've no authority . . .' she started to say, but he interrupted impatiently.

'Haven't I? You may be employed by Summer Canvas but this site is mine and I have the final say on all personnel who work here.'

There was a taunting finality in his tone and manner which both hurt and irked Alison. Could this be the same man who'd spoken to her so tenderly, who'd caressed her so intimately? He had become a stranger to her. No, worse than a stranger, because of what there had been between them. And yet as well as the hurt there was anger. How dared he make these assumptions, moral judgements about her? Judgements that could lose her her job?

'How dare you threaten me, you . . . you pompous prig?' The words were out before she could stop them.

Max threw back his dark head and laughed. 'Your English insults won't have any effect on me.'

'I'll try a few French ones, then,' Alison muttered scathingly, fishing round in her mind for a few choice French words that would effectively convey her indignation, but finding none strong enough for what she wanted to say. A pity secretarial college hadn't offered a course on insults for arrogant Frenchmen.

Abruptly Max stopped laughing. 'Forget the jokes, Alison. You've proved yourself irresponsible and I don't want you on this site any longer.'

'But you're jumping to all the wrong conclusions. You don't even know what happened,' Alison protested.

'I didn't need to draw conclusions, I had evidence. I was there, remember.' Max drawled insolently.

Alison shook her head, dazed by the rapid course events were taking. Last night had been bad enough, but now this as well. 'Please, Max, just let me explain.'

'There's nothing to explain. You *entertained* your lover while you were supposed to be babysitting, with disastrous consequences. That's all the explanation I need. I'm not interested in your excuses.'

Alison was incensed at the insult. Instinctively her hand came up to slap his face. Her reactions were swift but Max's were quicker, and his own hand rose to pinion hers in mid-air. The next second they were wrapped in an ungainly struggle. The movement unbalanced Alison and the next moment she found herself toppling into the pool, Max with her. The shock of the cold water brought them both to their senses, and as soon as they surfaced they both struck out for the sides. Max hauled himself out first and then put out his hand to pull Alison out.

Afterwards she wasn't quite sure what happened next; one minute she was standing beside the pool dripping wet, her hand still in Max's, acutely conscious of his proximity and his touch, yet equally aware there was no tenderness in it for her. The next moment he was pulling her against him, his mouth closing on hers with rough, demanding urgency.

Alison made to pull away from him, but his hand left hers to arc round her back, pulling her against him with a possessiveness which brooked no resistance.

Twisting her head from side to side, she tried to evade the cruel savagery of his mouth, but his other hand came up to bury itself in her hair, forcing her head still for his assault.

This wasn't lovemaking, but a cruel parody of what there had been between them during the previous week. Until now, Max's lovemaking had taken her every step of the way with him, insistent but not forceful, demanding but not extorting, exciting but never violating. What he was doing to her now shocked her. She could feel the muscular sinews of his thighs against hers, the compact hardness of his torso against her body, the tough resilience of male chest-hair against her breasts. Every part of her seemed to be in contact with his maleness, but it was a maleness which sought neither to accommodate nor embrace, merely to dominate with its impermeable strength.

For one horrible moment she thought she couldn't breathe, that she was going to faint against Max's bruising mouth, his body's searing toughness. And then, as if by magic, the pressure ceased. Max the skilful lover replaced this brutal stranger. Max, who knew every responsive recess of her mouth, every throbbing pulse in her throat, every sensitive curve and hollow. From close to unconsciousness, Alison abruptly found herself only too conscious of what was happening to her.

A gush of warmth spread upwards from her thighs, curling her stomach in delicious tendrils and swelling her breasts, making her nipples harden with undeniable pleasure against Max's chest. Her mouth ceased to struggle for evasion, seeking instead to invite his tongue to ever-deeper liberties.

Hands left the small of her back to explore the rounded contours of her buttocks, leaving a trail of heated flesh, inadequately protected by the swimsuit's flimsy material.

For a few breathtaking moments she thought that everything was all right between them, that her body had silently communicated the truth of last night to Max and that he somehow, intuitively, understood its message. But when he abruptly pulled away from her, putting his hands to her shoulders to thrust her from him with harsh indifference, his eyes spelt a different message. Even while they glittered with

desire, they stripped every shred of respect from her
with contemptuous insolence. 'What a convincing
performance, Alison. You're a very accomplished
little actress altogether, aren't you? All that talk about
needing time . . . you even had me convinced, and I
thought I was immune to such wiles. But don't think
this little display will work with me. Enticing though
your charms are, I can't wait to see the back of them.'

If Max had struck her, Alison couldn't have been
more shocked by what he said. Every word pierced
like a dagger blow. She stumbled backwards away
from him, just as if he had hit her. Then, without
even pausing to collect her sandals or towel, she
turned from him and fled back to the tent, tears
coursing down her cheeks.

Jane was awake when Alison returned. 'Where
have . . .?' she began, and then, seeing Alison's
dishevelled state, 'Alison, what on earth's
happened?'

For several minutes Alison couldn't speak as sobs
racked her body. Despair engulfed her. She had
never, ever imagined Max capable of such cruelty.

Jane shook her gently, begging Alison to tell her
what had happened. Pride alone forbade that she
told even Jane of Max's final thrust, that hurt was
hers alone to bear. 'I've . . . I've just seen Max . . . he
says I've got to leave . . . because . . . because of last
night.' The words came out in shuddering gasps.

'Oh, no!' Jane's arm was immediately round
Alison's shoulders. 'It's all my fault. I'll go and see
him straight away. If one of us has to leave, it's going
to be me. Last night wasn't your fault.'

'No.' Alison's tear-stained face lifted. 'No, I think it

would be better if I did go.' She couldn't tell Jane the
whole truth about Max, about what had just
happened between them. She wasn't even sure what
the whole truth about Max was now. She'd been
angry when he'd made the unjust accusations. Angry
that he had condemned her without even hearing
what she had to say. But that anger was nothing to
the pain she had felt when he had insulted her so
cruelly.

Jane's face was unhappy and concerned. 'Alison,
please, this is ridiculous. It is all my fault, I should
have said something last night.'

'No, honestly,' Alison started to protest, but this
time Jane was firm.

'No, it is my fault and I'm not allowing you to take
the blame. If one of us has to leave, it's going to be
me.'

When Jane had gone, Alison shrugged off her wet
swimsuit with fumbling, uncooperative fingers and
put on clean jeans and a blouse. Then she started to
gather together her belongings. Whatever the
outcome of Jane's visit to Max, she couldn't stay
here. Not after what had happened this morning.

About an hour later, Helen put her head round the
corner of door-flap and smiled encouragingly. 'The
Comte wants to see you in the manager's office.'

The hundred-yard journey seemed endless as her
feet dragged like dead weights every step of the way,
and, entering the manager's office, Alison felt more
nervous than she had ever done when taking exams.
As well as the manager, the Davisons were there and
Simon and Jane . . . and Max. Alison refused to look
at him, but was forced to when he addressed her

directly, wasting no time in getting straight to the point.

'It seems you were wrongly blamed last night for Kim's disappearance. In fact you were not babysitting at all.'

Alison nodded wearily. 'That's right. But the responsibility is still mine. I shouldn't have left Kim at all.'

Max's eyes were veiled shafts of green. 'I agree,' he concurred smoothly, 'you shouldn't have left her. Nevertheless, you weren't the one with her when she actually disappeared.'

'No, I wasn't.' Alison's chin lifted defiantly.

'Then why on earth didn't you say so at the time?' he demanded, a shade less smoothly.

'You didn't give me any opportunity,' she retorted swiftly. 'And besides,' she added more quietly, conscious that there were others in the room besides herself and Max, 'it didn't seem so important at the time. The main concern was to find Kim.'

At this point Mr Davison interrupted. 'Please, Comte Belreynac, if I may say something, I know what happened last night upset us all terribly . . .' he squeezed his wife's hand '. . . but Kim was found safely in the end. Miss Fraser here . . .' he regarded Jane with some disapproval '. . . has explained what happened and, while I can't approve of what was going on, I must say that Kim was at fault as well. She's been told never to leave the tent without us, especially at night, so she was somewhat to blame too. My wife and I feel that this has been upsetting enough for everyone concerned. We don't want it to go any further.'

Max's glance travelled across the group of people in the office. There was an air of suspense as everyone waited to hear what he would say. 'Under the circumstances, that is very generous, Mr Davison. I think, from what Miss Fraser has said, that last night's incident is never likely to be repeated and so, since it is your express request, no further action will be taken.'

There was an almost audible sigh of relief from everyone. Despite the trauma and upset of the night before, it was obvious that the Davisons had no desire to carry the issue further. Having been assured that the occurrence would not be repeated, they were content to let it rest.

From the site manager's point of view, it was clearly better for business to let the matter drop than to have one of the couriers sent home in disgrace. His expression positively oozed *bonhomie*.

And as for Jane and Simon, their own sense of guilt had punished them far more than any external pressure could have done, and they were infinitely grateful to the Davisons for responding as they had.

As Alison glanced round at the other people in the room, their faces clearly registered their various reactions. It was not difficult to interpret how they were feeling. All except Max. His face was an inscrutable mask and Alison had no idea whether he was feeling satisfaction, good-will, relief, or anything at all.

After a few minutes, the group started to move towards the door, ready now to put last night behind them and get on with the day's normal routine. For them it was all over, best forgotten. Alison tried to look as if she shared their feelings, but knew that none of their reactions coincided with hers. Relief yes, but she had felt that last night when Kim was found safely. This morning all she felt was the hurt and pain Max had inflicted. None of what had been said in this office had eased that. She was almost at the door when Max's voice carried across to her. 'I'd like you to stay behind for a few minutes, Alison.'

Would he, indeed? Alison felt like sticking her tongue out and telling him exactly what he could do with his wishes. But, of course, that would have looked rather odd, childish behaviour to the rest of the company. Instead she deferred politely and turned back into the room.

Max must have had a discreet word with Alain, too, because he left along with the others, muttering something about having to check the launderette.

For several minutes she and Max eyed each other silently over the desk; he sitting back in the swivel chair on the other side of it, twirling a pencil between his fingers, she sitting primly on the edge of her upright chair, deliberately waiting for him to make the first move. He'd asked her to stay behind, let him do the talking.

'Why didn't you tell me, Alison?'

She didn't need to ask what he was talking about. 'You didn't give me a chance,' she replied candidly.

Max shook his head. '*Mon Dieu*, Alison, there had to be some moment, last night . . . this morning, when you could have told me.'

Alison's gaze held his steadily. 'Do you really believe that? If you do, you're deluding yourself. I tried to explain but you wouldn't listen, you didn't want to listen. You believed what you wanted to believe. It wasn't strength of mind on your part, it was sheer, arrogant obstinacy.'

Abruptly Max put down the pencil, got up from his chair and moved round to her side of the desk, resting his hip on its edge. 'You must admit the evidence looked pretty damning.'

'OK, I'll admit it *appeared* pretty bad. But if you'd scratched beneath the surface you'd have discovered it wasn't true.'

Max gave a mock wince, though his eyes were serious. 'I think I owe you an apology.'

Alison wished he wasn't so close to her, within touching distance. His proximity did strange things to her thought processes, making them confused and illogical instead of coherent and logical as she wanted them to be. Under the chair, she pressed her heels against its lower bar, using its solidity to prop up her resolve. 'You may be able to apologise for your error, but nothing you could say could undo those accusations you made this morning. Have you any idea how you made me feel?' she demanded coldly.

Easing his hip further on to the desk, Max moved perceptibly closer. The bunched muscles of his thigh, taut beneath the fabric of his trousers, held her eyes as if by magnetism. Frantically Alison tugged her gaze away from them, searching his frame for some less evocative area to focus on, but finding none. After everything he'd said earlier, she still couldn't deny the sexual pull which he held for her.

'Alison, look at me,' he commanded softly. 'I should never have said those things, they were cruel and unjust.'

Was it possible to drown when you weren't anywhere near water? Max's eyes weren't cold and savage like the ocean now; they were the inviting green of coastal waters, gently lulling. How very easy it would be to immerse oneself in them. Alison tried to transfix her eyes on the knot of Max's tie, it seemed about the safest area of his anatomy right now. 'You . . . you can't just *unsay* something like that. You did say it and I can't just forget it.'

Max's hand came down to take hers, pulling her up to stand between his legs and hooking his hands round her lower back, as his eyes and his voice caressed her. 'Sometimes actions can speak louder then words. Don't you agree? Let me show you how sorry I am,' and his mouth came down to nuzzle the soft skin of her throat, seeking out its pulse-spots with his tongue.

Alison closed her eyes to try to block the exquisite sensations beginning to course through her veins. 'I don't know,' she murmured ineffectually.

Max's mouth extended its investigations to her lobes, nipping the tender flesh gently between his teeth. 'But I know,' he muttered softly against her ear. 'Trust me.'

When his fingers came up to undo the buttons of her blouse with slow, deliberate intent, she did nothing to stop him, feeling the warmth of his hands against the bare flesh of her midriff as inch by inch her blouse parted at his insistence. The air between them seemed charged and, when her eyes opened to encounter his, Alison wondered when she had ever felt more erotically feminine. Despite the inappropriate setting, the hour of the morning, she felt that languorous heat which was a prelude to lovemaking wash over her in warm, enticing waves.

Infinitely slowly, Max's mouth lowered to nuzzle the V of her breasts erupting between the lacy cups of her bra, running his tongue over their creamy fullness until her nipples strained against their soft enclosures.

Why struggle against this tidal wave inside her? It was a losing battle, every sensory defence was being swept aside by Max's invasion. Weakly Alison arched against him, exulting in the raw masculinity she encountered there, evidence of his own arousal.

'And you're not going to leave?' Max demanded, his mouth now just inches away from - hers, capitalising on her surrender.

'What?' Alison opened her eyes. Leave? Jane must have told Max she was planning to go. Good grief! Jonathon! He said he'd come for her, to take her back. She'd forgotten. She was supposed to be meeting him for lunch to talk about it. Oh, God! How could she have let this happen?

The sudden influx of reality caused Alison to suddenly stiffen in Max's arms, no longer yielding and bemused.

'I . . . er . . . I don't know.' The words were strangled with uncertainty.

Max's hands dropped from her waist, though his eyes held hers steadily. 'What exactly don't you know?'

'I don't know if I shall stay,' she answered, despair cutting into her voice as jellylike fingers tried to remedy her exposure.

'Because of this morning?'

'Partly,' she dissembled.

'Or because of your English *friend?*' Max
emphasised the term.

'I've got to talk to him, Max,' Alison begged for his
understanding. She at least had to talk to Jonathon.
To resolve their relationship one way or another.

'Of course you must,' Max agreed smoothly,
dangerously, at the same time putting her from him
gently but firmly and returning to his former side of
the desk. Once more he was the boss and she merely
the employee.

'If you do decide to go, please let me know.' His
voice was as cool as chipped ice, as if the passion of a
few minutes ago had never existed.

'Of course,' Alison agreed quietly, and turned to
go. There was so much more she wanted to say, but
how? Max had turned again into a polite, remote
stranger and she had no idea how to reach him.

Jonathon had hired a car, and when he picked Alison
up at lunch time they both agreed it would be better
to leave the site for a few hours in order to talk, rather
than attract inquisitive attention. Alison knew that
the other couriers, most of whom were aware of her
relationship with Max, would be curious about the
unexpected arrival of another 'man in her life'.

They drove to the nearby town of Beynat for lunch
and then parked the car beside the Dordogne river,
walking down to its sandy banks and settling
themselves in a grassy nook.

All the time she was beside him, in the car and in
the restaurant, Alison eyed Jonathon covertly
beneath her lashes. He was as good-looking as ever,

and his particular brand of extrovert charm attracted a good many slyly smiling glances from females, old and young. Alison kept waiting for it to have the effect on her it had once done. But it didn't happen. She was still aware of it, it was too blatant to pass unnoticed, but in a dispassionate, detached sort of way. She seemed to have developed a personal immunity to it and this in itself came as a shock. She had been so strongly captivated by Jonathon's charms during their relationship, and in his absence had perhaps even magnified them, that now, confronted by the reality, she wasn't entirely sure why they had so little impact.

But if she remained politely impassive, Jonathon didn't appear to notice, seeming not to need her active adulation for him to believe it still existed. All during lunch he kept the conversation going, deliberately steering it away from personal topics and on to more general ones—work and home mainly—filling her in on news of past colleagues and mutual friends. It was all very pleasant and undemanding, but after a while Alison found herself getting restless and fidgety. She and Jonathon were like two distant relatives, skating politely over cordial matters. This couldn't be why he'd come all this way to see her, and certainly wasn't why she had agreed to see him. They had to *talk*, really talk. About themselves, not other people.

'How did you find me?' she asked as they started on their coffee, attempting to bring the conversation into more personal realms.

'Not now, sweetheart.' He patted her hand. 'Wait till we're on our own.'

The pat on her hand felt patronising, and why didn't the prospect of being alone with Jonathon fill her with any particular pleasure, as it undoubtedly would have done a few months ago?

An hour later, stretched out on the grassy bank, she repeated the question. Jonathon stroked a piece of reed thoughtfully between his fingers. 'Annabel told me in the end. Your mother was furious with me, wouldn't even let me in the house, said I'd broken your heart and wasn't the poor girl entitled to some peace? Did I break your heart, sweetheart?' he asked, not looking entirely displeased at the prospect.

Alison sifted sand through her fingers, pondering the question as if it were of incalculable significance. She'd certainly *thought* Jonathon had broken her heart, that day at the flat and for some months afterwards. Yet here it was, beating away nicely and not even fluttering faintly at the memory. Was it her heart which had been bruised or just her pride? 'No, you didn't break my heart,' she answered honestly. Maybe battered it a little, like an egg, she felt like adding, but decided Jonathon wouldn't appreciate the humour right now.

'Oh, good,' he murmured, somewhat unconvincingly.

Is that it? Alison wondered. Did he come all this way simply to check if my heart was still intact? Rather late for surgery, she thought flippantly. Why was she feeling so facetious? It wasn't like her.

Jonathon cleared his throat as if he were about to say something of great import. 'I think you were a bit hard on me, Alison . . . back in England.'

Alison's eyebrows rose incredulously. 'You think *I* was hard on *you* . . . You were the one in bed with that . . . that woman, remember?' The kid gloves were well and truly off now.

Jonathon smiled with just the right touch of remorse. 'Sweetheart, you know that didn't mean anything to me. It was just a bit of fun . . . a game.'

'Fun and games are for children, Jonathon. Not grown-ups,' Alison bit back tartly.

'OK, I was a naughty boy. But I've learnt my lesson, it won't happen again. Can't you forgive me?' He smiled endearingly, apparently believing that a few contrite words were all it would take to put the clock back on their relationship.

Alison wondered what he expected her to do—give him a sharp rap on the knuckles and forget about it? If he'd said all this at the time, wasn't that what she would have done? 'Why have you suddenly decided to tell me all this now? Why not at the time?' she asked curiously.

Jonathon shrugged. 'Pride, I guess. You gave me quite a shock that day, walking in like that. I needed a bit of time to get over it.'

'And when *you'd* got over the shock of the experience, you came looking for me and I wasn't there,' Alison suggested, beginning to fit the pieces of the puzzle together.

'I just didn't expect you to up and leave like that. Work, yes, it was getting a bit awkward working together anyway, but I didn't expect you to leave England, too.'

'Perhaps I should have left a forwarding address, just so you could have contacted me, only if you'd wanted to, of course,' Alison suggested drily.

'Don't be sarcastic, it doesn't suit you,' Jonathon reproved.

'And what does suit me? Do you know, do you even care, Jonathon?' Alison demanded, her eyes glinting like shining chestnuts.

'I thought we suited each other,' Jonathon murmured a little sulkily.

'I thought so too, but I didn't need a change of partner in my bed just to be sure. It doesn't seem to matter to you, Jonathon, that you betrayed me, deceived me behind my back. How do you think I felt that day? Have you tried to understand *my* feelings in all this?'

Jonathon tugged hard at the reed, breaking it. 'Would I be here now if I didn't care about you, Alison? I never wanted us to finish.'

Alison shook her head. 'Don't you realise that makes it even worse? You wanted the best of both worlds. Me and that woman, or someone else like her. Life's not like that, Jonathon. Grown-ups can't be like children, wanting everything they see in the toy shop. They have to make choices and stick by them.'

'Good God! You've turned into quite a little moraliser, haven't you, Alison? What is it, something in the air down here?'

Alison's expression was grave, though her eyes had lost their hard glitter. 'No, I've just grown up enough to realise that a lot of charm served up with a few candlelit dinners doesn't add up to love.'

'Meaning?' Jonathon glowered at her.

'Meaning you and I have nothing more to say to

each other.' And this time she really meant it.

'Do you mean to say I've come all this way for nothing? You're not going to come back with me?' Jonathon looked astonished.

''Fraid so,' Alison nodded, quite enjoying herself now. For the first time in months, she felt truly liberated. It had taken the separation from Jonathon and then meeting him again for her to realise just what sort of man he was. Charming, handsome, successful, yes . . . but also spoiled, self-centred and immature. She hadn't been in love with him, she'd been in love with the idea of being in love. She'd become so obsessed with the idea of marriage and settling down that she'd lost sight of the man himself. Jonathon would never really care about anyone except himself, and that sort of egotism made a poor foundation for any relationship, let alone marriage.

The journey back to the camp-site was a mainly silent one. Out of politeness Alison did ask what Jonathon's plans were now, and was coolly informed that as soon as he had dropped her off and collected his belongings from the hotel in Sarlat he would head up to Paris. Alison smiled to herself. She had no doubt that Jonathon would find ample consolation in the arms of some delectable Parisienne.

The tent was deserted when she returned, and Alison assumed that Jane and Simon were spending the afternoon together. Since it was a Saturday and there were no jobs to be dealt with, Alison decided she might as well enjoy what was left of the afternoon sunshine.

After unfolding the lounger and sorting herself out with sunglasses and a cool drink, she settled back on the padded material. She felt tired after the lack of sleep the night before, but her mind was too full to relax into unconsciousness. So much had happened in the last twenty-four hours, it seemed as if weeks had gone by and she felt as if she were living in the jumbled world of Mr Topsy-Turvy, one of the Mr Men and a great favourite with her youngest nephew, her sister Annabel's son.

The realisation that she didn't love Jonathon, had never really loved him, hadn't been as much of a shock as she had expected. Perhaps her heart had known for some time, but she'd been so infatuated with her memories that she hadn't heard it. It was easier to understand her relationship with Jonathon in retrospect. She had been flattered when Jonathon first sought her out—after all, he was one of the rising stars in the company—and they'd had enough in common to form a passable relationship. But she'd wanted more than that—perhaps she was just ready to fall in love. After all, her parents were happily married and she had two sisters and a brother all happily married; maybe her biological clock had suddenly decided it was her turn and she'd simply homed in on the first eligible male in her path. That might have been OK, except that she'd become so engrossed in the fantasy that she'd lost sight of the reality, of the type of man Jonathon was. Marriage would never have worked between them, she knew that now. It would have had a superficial, glossy veneer but no substance beneath it.

It was all so clear now, so obvious; why hadn't it

been before? She'd wasted weeks dwelling on her feelings for Jonathon, when really she should have been . . . what? Dwelling on her feelings for Max? Why had she suddenly had such crystal-clear insight into the shallowness of Jonathon's character? It wasn't Jonathon alone who had exposed his own weakness, but his comparison with Max. At first she'd thought they had so much in common—good looks, charm, success—and she'd been frightened that she'd only been attracted to Max on the rebound from Jonathon, thinking that it was impossible for her to care deeply for Max because she still loved Jonathon. What a fool she'd been. Her heart had been trying to guide her there, too, and she hadn't listened to it. She wasn't simply attracted to Max. She loved him.

The realisation was so abrupt that Alison opened her eyes wide against the glare of the sun. 'I love Max.' She said it slowly, out loud, and as she said it every inch of her being, mind, body and soul, endorsed the statement's validity. All at once Alison knew beyond any shadow of doubt that what she felt for Max wasn't the infatuation she'd felt for Jonathon, but the love of a woman for a man.

On a superficial level the two men were similar, but on a deeper level they had nothing in common. Whereas Jonathon lived for himself with little thought or concern for anyone else, only seeing others of value if they enhanced his glory or flattered his ego, Max was a man in every sense of the word. Attractive and confident, yes, but also sure of his own identity—he had no need to use others merely as reflectors of his own conceit. He knew what he wanted and aimed for it, but not at the expense of others. Above all, he cared about other people—Cécile, his late father, his workers, the holiday-makers, Kim last night—in a way that Jonathon never could.

Yet, for all his strengths, Max wasn't perfect. He was capable of error, of losing his temper—as he had done this morning. But he was a strong enough character to recognise those errors and apologise for them. Wasn't that the true essence of strength of character? To be able to admit your mistakes. With Jonathon, she had seen none of his failings and weakness, her love had been illusory and unreal because it hadn't been able to admit any flaws in its object. With Max, she saw his faults and his strengths and loved the whole man they constituted, not some unreal figment of her imagination.

But where exactly did this startling revelation get her? It was all very well pondering on her feelings for Max in an academic context, when in reality she'd all but thrown their relationship away after their cool parting this morning. As far as Max was concerned, she had rejected the olive branch he had extended in favour of Jonathon, and she knew he had too much pride to extend it again. You fool, she berated herself miserably; if only you'd listened to your heart instead of heeding some misplaced notion of loyalty to Jonathon. She'd sorted Jonathon out well enough, and thrown everything else into chaos as a consequence.

Perhaps it was about time she started extending a few olive twigs of her own. There was no reason nowadays why a woman shouldn't do a little manipulating, and surely if she explained to Max . . . not everything, of course, but simply that Jonathon had gone away and she had stayed, then Max could draw his own conclusions?

There would be a disco in the bar tonight. With a bit of luck, Max would be there, and if she just happened to be there too . . . well, it was worth a try.

Several hours later Alison entered the bar accompanied by Jane, Simon, Matthew and, amazingly enough, Helen and David. There was just one alcove left unoccupied at the far end of the room and they all squeezed themselves into it like sardines. Very cosy, thought Alison drily, finding herself thigh to thigh with David. For once he seemed surprisingly chatty. 'Any more incidents reported?' he enquired of no one in particular.

'Such as?' Jane asked bluntly. She didn't like David and made no bones about showing it.

He waved his hand in the air, expounding vaguely. 'Oh, you know, thefts, minor damage, that sort of thing.'

Simon shrugged. 'We had a new one today. Car tyres slashed . . . ruined, all of them. The owner was furious, and I can't say I blame him.'

'Did you report it?' Alison asked, trying to sound casual, yet thinking immediately that Max should know about it.

Simon nodded. 'We told Alain, but there's not a lot he can do about it. It probably happened in the night.'

'Did he mention whether or not they're planning to set up any sort of night watch . . . since most of these . . . er . . . incidents seem to occur at night?' The question came from David.

Grinning, Simon shook his head. 'What? A sort of home guard, you mean? You can have first go with the cannon, David.'

David gave a tight-lipped smile, though Alison felt him shift uncomfortably beside her.

'Have you had any strange incidents occurring?' she asked thoughtfully.

This time it was Helen who answered. 'You bet. I had a woman up in arms last week because her heated rollers had been taken . . . said it would ruin her holiday if she couldn't do her hair . . . I ask you.' And she rolled her eyes expressively.

'Though that's nothing compared with your little escapade last night, is it?' David suggested, an unpleasant smirk on his face.

'Meaning?' Alison eyed him coolly.

'Well, I don't imagine Summer Canvas are going to be very pleased when they learn you managed to mislay a child between you.'

'Were you planning to tell them?' Alison asked solemnly.

David cleared his throat. 'No . . . er . . . of course not. But I'm sure the parents will.'

'That will be the Davisons' business, not yours,' Alison concluded drily.

Looking distinctly peeved, David raised his glass and downed its contents, then got up to get a refill, not even bothering to ask anyone else if they would like another drink. Jane pulled a face at his departing back. 'What a misery that man is. Pity we couldn't manage to mislay *him* for the rest of the summer!' The rest of the group giggled and the cloud of tension lifted.

As the evening progressed Alison found herself looking at her watch more and more frequently. By the time it got to eleven o'clock, she'd almost given up hope of Max appearing. Although the disco went on until well after midnight, it seemed unlikely that he'd arrive so late. Matthew was regaling them all with an incredibly boring explanation of the plumbing problems faced by an extensive site like Belreynac, totally oblivious to the stifled yawns and shuffling feet of the others.

By eleven-thirty, Alison had had enough. Max wasn't going to come, and if she heard one more reference to ball valves and drain cocks she thought she'd scream. Waiting for a suitable break in the monologue to mutter her farewells, she heard David give a low wolf-whistle under his breath. That anything or anyone could make David wolf-whistle aroused her curiosity in itself, and her eyes followed the direction of his gaze. How she wished they hadn't!

Standing at the doorway was Max with two couples . . . and another woman, clearly his female companion for the evening. There could be no possibility that she was his sister this time. Tall, blonde and willowy, she looked like a model, all sleek curves and bloodstock lines. The plunging neckline of her dress was what had attracted David's attention and, judging by the admiring glances which followed her passage across the floor, most of the other males present as well. But it wasn't her neckline Alison was interested in. It was her red, pouting lips as she smiled up at Max, and her long, red fingernails as she hooked her arm gracefully through his. Her eyes watched their progress as if mesmerised, watched the way Max inclined his dark head to her blonde one, watched the way his hard mouth curved with amusement at something she said, watched the way his hand slid familiarly round her slender waist as he eased her into a corner seat beside him.

All the time her eyes watched, a cold hand seemed to take a grip on her heart and squeeze it painfully. She'd thought it amusing earlier to discover how steady her heartbeat remained in Jonathon's presence; now it felt as if it was being shattered into a thousand tiny splinters. Only this morning, those same hands had been on her waist, those same lips on her mouth, his eyes had communicated the same intimacy to her that they now communicated to this woman.

'Well, well, the Comte certainly has a way with women. That one's positively eating out of his hand . . . Not that he seems exactly resistant to *her* charms, either.' David deliberately pushed the knife in deeper, glad of an opportunity to repay Alison for her earlier gibes.

'Shut up, David. You've about as much charm as a rattlesnake and as much tact as a rhinoceros. When we want your opinion we'll ask for it.' Loyally Jane leapt to her friend's defence.

Eyes bright with unshed tears, Alison smiled gratefully. She dared not speak because she knew that, if she did, the floodgates would open. All she wanted to do was get out of here and back to the tent, to be left alone to lick her wounds in peace.

To get to the door, she had to cross the entire width

of the dance area in the centre. Inevitably Max would
see her, would know that she had seen him, but
Alison didn't care. All she wanted to do was get out
with her pride intact.

It was only a short walk, some thirty yards, but it
might as well have been thirty miles. Alison
measured every footfall, every square tile of flooring.
Then at last it was over. She was outside and running
as if her life depended on it back to the tent. Only
then, in the privacy of her small, fabric sleeping
compartment did the tears come, and she sobbed as if
her heart would break.

CHAPTER NINE

IN THE week that followed, Alison worked and felt like someone only half alive. She went about her chores as if on automatic pilot, getting them done because they had to be done, but taking little pleasure or interest in them any more. The children noticed a difference during the morning sessions and started playing up. At first Alison was irked that even they seemed intent on causing her further problems, but she soon realised it was their way of getting her attention, trying to break through the despondent, indifferent shroud of apathy which seemed to surround her. She made an effort to pull herself together for their sake and concentrate on the activities, but her heart wasn't in it and the children knew it.

One of the worst moments had been saying goodbye to Cécile. Cécile's mother had collected her on the Sunday afternoon and had deliberately stopped by at the tent on her departure to thank Alison for allowing Cécile to participate in the games sessions and say how much her daughter had enjoyed them. Alison appreciated the gesture, but any gratification was overshadowed by the memories of how happy the previous weeks had been when she and Cécile and Max had spent so much time in each other's company and the awareness that they could never now be repeated.

'Give Uncle Max a kiss from me,' had been Cécile's parting words, and of course the child had no idea how much pain her simple request had conjured up. Alison coloured with embarrassment as her mother looked from Cécile to Alison with speculative interest. Whatever her surmise of her daughter's comment, she tactfully sidestepped any awkwardness by remarking on how much Cécile's English had improved during her stay. Finally the black car slid away and Alison was left staring after it as her last link with Max disappeared into the distance.

Automated though all her external actions had become, Alison's emotions underwent a profound change during the course of the week. At first there had just been an all-engulfing pain, acutely focused on the image of Max with that woman. Then had come anger. Anger that he should cast her aside so quickly and easily, making advances to her and then, only hours later, finding a replacement—just as Jonathon had done. But finally her reaction had settled somewhere between the pain and the anger. Alison was too just to regard Max's behaviour through such distorted lenses for long. How could she blame him for what he had done? He hadn't deceived her behind her back as Jonathon had, he hadn't made promises and then broken them. He'd asked her to stay at Belreynac and indirectly he had been asking her if she was willing to give their relationship another chance. It was she who'd backed away from that commitment, she who'd insisted on seeing Jonathon before she could give him an answer. She who'd left Max with the impression that

Jonathon meant more to her than he did. After that, was it really any wonder Max had shifted his attentions to a female so much more obviously enamoured of his charms?

It didn't help to know that things could perhaps have been different if she had behaved differently, if she had only realised sooner that it was Max she loved, not Jonathon. How could she have been so blind?

By the following weekend Alison felt limp and exhausted. She had caught sight of Max occasionally during the week, but never close enough to talk to, and what could she have said to him if they had spoken? She had not seen him again with the blonde woman but, since she had not been back to the bar since that evening, she couldn't be sure whether the woman was still in circulation or not. Certainly Jane hadn't mentioned anything, but that might have been tact on her part, and Alison hadn't had the courage to ask.

On the Saturday evening there was to be an open-air barbecue to welcome the latest batch of new arrivals. It was the last sort of function Alison felt like attending, but all the couriers were expected to be there. Jane, Simon and Matthew had volunteered to spend the afternoon preparing for it, lugging bales of straw from the barns to the terraced areas beyond the swimming pool. Not feeling like joining in with their bubbly good humour, Alison had offered to clean out the six tents being vacated that morning and prepare them for the new arrivals due later in the afternoon. Cleaning and re-stocking tents was one of those monotonous task which couriers had to do over and over again during the summer period, the job becoming less and less popular with repetition. Certainly Jane was only too glad to leave that particular chore to her.

By about three o'clock the tents were all finished, sparkling clean and stocked with basic grocery items—sugar, tea, coffee, milk, loaf of bread, butter and cheese, so that even if new holiday-makers arrived after the shop had closed for the evening they could at least make themselves a drink and a snack.

Zipping up the last door-flap behind her, Alison stretched her arms in the air and arched her back. She felt stiff after bending and crouching to sweep in corners and sort out sleeping compartments. Further down the line of tents she passed David, engaged in the same job she'd just completed. He looked hot and dusty, his neck an ugly red colour.

'Hi,' she acknowledged as she passed, not slowing her footsteps. She and David had nothing to say to each other. It was David who put out his hand to detain her.

'Finished your tents, have you?'

Alison nodded, at the same time glancing down at his hand on her arm. He let it drop away. 'Yes, I've finished them. Why?' she answered evenly. It wasn't like David to be so conversational.

He shook his head indifferently. 'No reason, just asking. Are you going to the barbecue tonight?'

Alison nodded again. 'We're all going, aren't we?'

David smiled, except it wasn't a smile, it was a smirk. 'I just thought you seemed to have gone out of circulation this past week. Ever since our friend the Comte found himself another playmate.'

Alison's hands itched to wipe the sneer off his face, but she refused to let him see the pain his words inflicted. Opening her eyes wide, she enquired with mock innocence, 'Playmate? I didn't know there were going to be games tonight as well. Thanks for letting me know, David, I'd better hurry off and find myself a partner.'

The sneer froze on David's features, giving him a callous, ruthless look and making Alison dislike him more than ever. Without even waiting for him to reply, she turned and continued down the path towards the centre.

Later on, in the shower, Alison surveyed her features critically. She'd been neither sleeping nor eating very well this week, and as a consequence dark shadows showed beneath her eyes and the delicate bone-structure of her face looked positively ethereal. Far from the glowing, healthy image she should be projecting, Summer Canvas's walking advertisement for life in the sun, she looked haggard and fragile. And no amount of fiddling with her hair this way or that way seemed to make any difference. At least when it had been long, its very bulk had added a rich vitality to her features. Now it seemed to droop dispiritedly along with the rest of her.

Back at the tent, she slapped on foundation and rouge indiscriminately. She still had some pride left. If Max was there tonight she didn't wanted to look as if she were pining with love before his very eyes. She might not be able to hide her feelings entirely, but at least she could camouflage their effects. After taking out the usual jeans and T-shirt from the hanging wardrobe, she changed her mind and selected instead a matching skirt and top. The skirt was full and flared, and the short-sleeved top loosely hugged her waist. The set had a bright pattern and at least gave the illusion of glowing cheerfulness.

Alison and Jane walked over to the barbecue area with Simon and Matthew. Regular site workers were dealing with the catering, so all they had to do was welcome new arrivals and make sure everyone seemed comfortable and relaxed.

The first hour or so was very busy as new people arrived, and all the couriers were busy circulating, ensuring that no one felt left out or isolated. After a while, though, most people seemed to settle down and started to form little groups among themselves, chatting and exchanging camping tips. By about ten o'clock the couriers were redundant and finally able to help themselves to glasses of wine and plates of steak and salad. A band were already tuning up, and it wouldn't be long before the grassy terraces were filled with swaying couples.

One of the families due that afternoon hadn't arrived, so before eating Alison made her way down to the gatehouse to see if any messages had been left. One had been pinned to the outside noticeboard, stating that the family's car had broken down at the ferry port and they wouldn't be arriving until the Sunday or Monday. Alison sympathised with their predicament, but there wasn't much she could do about it. At least she knew now the reason for their delay.

Back at the barbecue area, she toyed with the food on her plate, pushing it from one side to the other and not really eating anything. There was only one person she had any appetite for, and he wasn't on the menu tonight. Or any other night, for that matter, she reminded herself disconsolately. After about half an hour she found herself sitting alone; Simon and Jane were dancing and Matthew had gone off to find Helen. She suddenly realised how lonely it could be when the world around you seemed full of couples. Even David had found himself a dance partner, a rather plain teenager who gazed with cowlike docility into his stilted features. Alison watched them for a few minutes with half-hearted interest, curiosity vaguely aroused by the fact that anyone could find David appealing.

A shadow falling across the table made her glance up, and her heart did a triple somersault when she encountered Max standing there.

'Would you like to dance?'

The words implied she could refuse, but his voice told her he didn't expect her to.

Perhaps her pride should have been more assertive, but she couldn't deny the sudden rush of pleasure seeing him had provoked, nor the dictates of her body, which demanded she accept. When he led her on to the grassy terrace and drew her into his arms, she knew there was no other place in the whole world she would rather be, no other place it would feel so right to be.

No words came between them. There was only his hand on her waist, fingers just coming in contact with the bare flesh of her back beneath the loose-fitting top, her hand in his, and an acute awareness of his hard length moving rhythmically against her. It was a moment perfect in itself, needing neither past nor

future and requiring only that she submit herself
entirely to the sensations it invoked for the spell not
to be broken.

But enchantments rarely existed outside fairy-tales,
and as the music faded Max drew away from her,
breaking into the magic bubble which had briefly
surrounded them. 'You stayed.' The words cut
across the small distance between them.

Alison nodded silently. What could she say? I
didn't find anything worth leaving for after all, or, I
couldn't bear not to stay? Both true, and both
stripping her emotions of any protective layers.
Could she, should she, expose herself so candidly?

And yet an unspoken assent was all Max seemed to
need. The next moment he was taking her by the
hand and pulling her across the grassy banks, away
from the barbecue area, away from the other dancers,
and towards the château. Alison knew she could
have pulled her hand away, checked his advance, but
some force stronger than herself propelled her
forward unresisting. When they reached the château
grounds, Max drew her against the wall, leaning his
arms on either side of her, imprisoning her, and yet
did any prisoner acknowledge her constraint more
joyfully?

With a muffled groan he lowered his dark head to
hers, capturing her mouth and plundering its
softness with a sweet, bruising urgency. For seconds
. . . minutes, Alison had no idea how long, all was
mutual striving as mouths and tongues sought to
invade and capture, yield and assail, delight and
torment. It made no difference who was the
vanquished and who the victor.

And then, too soon, Max was pulling away from her, leaving her bereft and dissatisfied. When Alison opened her eyes to protest, Max's face was only inches away from hers, its hard lines uncompromising. 'You stayed. Why?' he demanded brusquely.

Alison's eyes were like two pools of melted chocolate, dark and warm, beseeching him to be tender with her. But Max was in no mood for tenderness right now. This girl . . . woman . . . had got under his skin. Far more than he'd ever intended her to. At first she'd roused his curiosity with her prickling defensiveness and the air of sadness which hung over her. But he'd always made it a policy never to get involved with the site workers or the couriers; it caused too many problems in the long run. Yet despite his reservations and against all his better judgement he'd found his interest in her growing. Why? She was attractive, yes, but certainly not the most beautiful woman he'd ever known. And definitely not the most amenable. After last Saturday he'd had enough. He'd vowed that was the end of it. Let her take up again with her English boyfriend and get off his site and out of his life for good. Yet here she was, still at Belreynac, and here he was, unaccountably undismayed at the knowledge. Why had she stayed? He had to know.

'Why did you stay, Alison?' He repeated the question, a shade more gently.

Alison looked beyond him to the starlit sky. Focusing on its black, diamond-studded infinity made honesty easier than when she stared into Max's dark, brooding features. 'I made a mistake. I didn't love

Jonathon. Seeing him . . . talking to him again made me see everything more clearly.' There was a quiet dignity in her voice and in the honesty of her words. Hadn't she herself said there was no shame, only strength, in being able to admit your mistakes?

'But why did you stay?' Max persisted ruthlessly, refusing to accept only half of her explanation, wanting, demanding that she admit the whole of it.

Alison's face turned back to his, lips trembling. 'Why do you think? Because I didn't want to leave you.' There, he had it all. Was he satisfied now?

Seemingly he was. The hard angles of his face softened and his eyes lost their glitter as his mouth descended on hers, tenderly exploring its softness and yielding mobility, as if to acknowledge it as the source of her surrender. But now Alison needed more than tenderness, she needed Max's strength and his vigour to affirm the rightness of her choice. Instinctively her hands sought the powerful muscles of his shoulders, one arm curling round his neck to allow her fingers the liberty of his hair, feeling its springy vitality beneath her fingers and urging his mouth to even deeper exploration of hers. She arched against him, feeling the solid firmness of his chest, his stomach, his thighs against her entire length.

Skilfully Max took the initiative, pushing her back gently against the wall to allow a small distance between them. Then his hand was on the bare flesh of her midriff, searing its softness with burning, trailing fingers which stroked and teased until her abdomen was a ball of molten flames licking and curling through her insides, making her whole being flame with desire. As his fingers skirted her ribcage,

Alison felt herself tauten with delighted anticipation, and, when Max adeptly unhooked the front fastening of her bra, swollen breasts welcomed their release. Supporting an aching fullness in the palm of his hand, Max's thumb circled its curve with taunting strokes before advancing to take possession of its erect peak between his fingers.

A moan of pleasure escaped Alison's lips, exposing the extent of her own arousal, and a moment later Max's lips had left hers to whisper huskily in her ear, 'I don't want to make love to you here. Come with me.'

Bemused and aroused as she was by Max's lovemaking, it took a few seconds for the full implication of his words to sink in. Instinctively her body went to follow his lead, but her mind drew back. Max had had his answer, but what about the questions she needed answers to? 'Max, please, I don't know if I'm ready,' she implored entreatingly, drawing her clothing back around her. Her body felt more alive than it had ever done but her mind felt numb and confused.

Max's voice, his hands, his body caressed her, sensing her need for reassurance. 'You're more than ready, darling; we both are,' he murmured gently.

Every physical instinct strained to endorse his words, but still her mind protested. 'Not physically . . . emotionally.' She begged for his understanding. 'That woman . . . last Saturday . . .' Alison couldn't go on with the question, and yet she had to know the answer. Much as she loved Max and desperately wanted, more than she'd ever wanted anything before, him to make love to her, she couldn't . . .

wouldn't allow to herself to become simply one more woman among many. In any relationship, married or otherwise, there had to be commitment and fidelity from both partners. If Max had made love to that woman last week then he couldn't make love to her now. Viewing sex as simply an enjoyable way of ending an evening, like having a brandy after a meal, devalued and debased it as far as she was concerned, and her own self-respect and principles could not permit it.

She didn't know how Max would react to her remarks. With anger, resentment, frustration perhaps. But she did know that she trusted him to be honest with her. If she did not trust him in that, there could be no basis for any relationship.

In fact Max's mouth curved in something resembling a smile and, when her eyes roamed over his face, she found no trace of anger, only faint amusement. 'What exactly did you want to know about *that woman?*' he demanded softly.

Alison's eyes searched his for some sign that he was playing with her, sporting with her emotions, but found none. 'You know what I'm asking,' she answered quietly.

'You're asking if I made love to her?' Unflinchingly Max put the question.

Holding his gaze, Alison nodded. 'I have to know, Max,' she whispered.

Max's voice was low and husky, revealing understanding but no embarrassment at the question. 'Several years ago, yes, Françoise and I were lovers. But I assure you, the sexual relationship between us was over a long time ago.'

His voice was mesmerising her, befuddling her senses. 'But she seemed so . . . so beautiful.' It was not what she had wanted to say at all. Françoise had certainly been beautiful, but she hadn't had the look of a platonic friend, more that of a woman intent on capturing her man. Surely Max must have seen it too?

If he had, he wasn't going to say. He smiled lazily, sending ripples of sheer pleasure down her spine. 'Françoise is very beautiful and very charming. We have remained friends—isn't that the way it should be?—but she arrived *and* departed on Saturday evening. I do not believe in casual sex, between past lovers or otherwise, Alison. Lovemaking is only enjoyable when both partners are willing to take time to explore each other's bodies, to understand each other's needs; it has to evolve and develop, would you not agree?'

How could she not agree when every inch of her body strained to get closer to Max, when every ounce of her being endorsed what he said? She'd had her answer, and she knew it to be an honest one.

A sudden night breeze chilled her bare arms and she gave an involuntary shiver. Max took her hand. 'Come,' he whispered.

Alison knew what he meant and this time didn't hesitate, for now she was ready. Holding his hand, she followed him towards the château.

Max's bedroom was huge and sumptuously furnished, but Alison barely noticed the furnishings or the décor. As soon as they entered the room, her eyes were drawn to the enormous bed at its far end and

then back to Max. She wanted Max to make love to
her, but that didn't prevent the rush of shyness
which seemed to engulf her now she found herself in
this overtly masculine domain. Immediately Max
drew her into his arms, allowing the strength of his
body to give the reassurances that no mere words
could.

Then he was picking her up in his arms and
carrying her across the room to the bed, depositing
her gently on to it but not allowing its covers to cool
her skin before he was beside her, his mouth
covering hers in a kiss which told her he would be as
demanding as he was tender, as passionate a lover as
he had once told her he would be. Alison felt no fear
at the prospect, only a mounting certainty that her
own desire would match his.

As Max deepened the kiss with consummate skill,
causing small gasps of pleasure to erupt in her throat,
Alison strove to extend the contact between them.
She needed to feel his skin, his warmth against her,
and her fingers started to fumble with the buttons of
his shirt, becoming exasperated with the numbness
of her fingers. Supporting himself on one elbow, Max
assisted her efforts, mouth curving with amusement
at her exasperation.

'It's all right, *chérie*, don't be so impatient. There's
no rush.'

Smiling back, Alison nodded, allowing her hands
to roam liberally over the muscled expanse of chest
above her, feeling the rough texture of its cloud of
hair with her fingers, and then exploring lower over
the taut muscles of his abdomen. With a muffled
groan, Max lowered his mouth to hers, probing its

depths and feeling her open herself to him. The eagerness of her response invited further liberties, and the next moment his hand was on her midriff, drawing sparks wherever it touched, lighting a fire which extended through her whole being. This time Alison helped him remove her top, unmindful of him seeing how shamelessly eager she was for his touch, and when his fingers released her bra she lay back on the bed, basking in the pleasure she saw her body gave him.

Max's hand cupped the swell of her breast, stroking its creamy smoothness tauntingly with his thumb until Alison arched towards him, knowing she would burst if he didn't ease the pressure soon. Just when she thought she could bear it no longer, Max lowered his mouth on to its taut peak, teasing the tiny mound with his tongue and then drawing it deep into his mouth. As though from miles away Alison heard herself moan with the exquisite sweetness of the sensation but, instead of releasing the pressure, it only pushed it to more demanding heights and she knew that soon all that would matter would be Max's body and her body and the satiation of the desires flooding through her like waves of an incoming tide upon the shore.

She gave a gasp of surprise when she felt Max's hand on the bare skin of her thigh, but his touch was firm and unhurried, exploring its lengthy expanse slowly until he was kneading the rounded curves of her buttocks, finding erogenous zones she had never known existed. No longer shy, Alison eased herself away from him slightly to wriggle out of the rest of her clothes, resentful even of that barrier between them. When she lay before him, naked and unashamed, his eyes spanned her slender length, their green depths warm with desire and promise for what lay ahead.

Within minutes Max was naked too and together they began to scale the delicious heights of exploration and discovery which lovers have shared since the beginning of time. Mouths kissing and whispering while hands roamed freely, delighting in the responses they roused and provoked. Finally, when Alison knew she could wait no longer, Max's hands gripped her writhing hips to hold her still for his possession, and rhythmically their bodies united as one, slowly at first and then more vigorously as both sought to invoke and bestow pleasure equally. Soon Alison found herself in a vortex of sensations, a whirlpool spinning her round and round, faster and faster, until her cries were mingling with Max's as they reached its centre together.

As dawn began to peer over the horizon, Alison turned in her sleep, unconsciously prodding Max with her elbow. The movement woke him and he shifted slightly to accommodate the female form beside him, then supported himself on the crook of his elbow to watch her as she slept. The sheet lay across her waist, but it was her face he examined, noting the relaxed innocence of her features, the way her lashes fanned smooth skin, the smattering of freckles on her cheeks which he hadn't noticed before, the gentle tilt of her nose, the generous curve of her lips. It was a face he could get used to seeing in the mornings and, he thought as his eyes flicked downwards, a body he could become used to making love to in the nights. Making love to her once hadn't been enough. Again last night he'd woken and been stirred by her feminine curves, caressing her into wakeful arousal, delighting in her uninhibited response. No, it would not be difficult to grow accustomed to such a woman. The direction his thoughts were taking caused a frown to flit across his features, but it lifted instantly as Alison, as if conscious of his appraisal, started to stir.

Alison yawned and stretched drowsily, opening her eyes to encounter Max's green ones smiling down at her. She smiled back languorously, recalling the passion of the night, the feel of his hands, the weight of his body on hers, the many words of lovers they had whispered to each other. There was no shame, no regret in the memory. She knew beyond any doubt that she loved Max, and, when such love existed, its expression could not be wrong.

'It's very early,' she said, noting that the dawn had still hardly penetrated the room.

'Very early,' Max agreed, his eyes not leaving hers.

'Too early to get up,' she suggested, lips curving provocatively.

'Much too early,' Max agreed mockingly, eyes glinting as he reached to pull her on top of him and moved beneath her in a way which showed exactly how they were going to welcome the new day.

Their lovemaking had just begun to deepen from playfulness into desire when there was an urgent tapping on the door. Max cursed under his beneath and glanced at his watch. Barely six o'clock! What the hell could Madame Chessaud want him for at this time of the morning?

'*Attendez un instant,*' he called brusquely, getting out of bed and going across to the adjacent dressing-room to pull on a towelling robe, before crossing to the door.

Left alone in the huge bed, Alison propped herself up on her elbows to try to hear what Max and Madame Chessaud were saying, but, since Max had closed the door ajar behind him to protect her from sight, all she could hear were their muffled voices and then a loud exclamation from Max.

Seconds later he was slamming the door shut behind him and striding back across the room. 'There's been an explosion,' he stated tersely, 'in one of the Summer Canvas tents.'

Alison stared at him disbelievingly. 'An explosion! Oh, God! Is anyone hurt?'

Max shook his head. 'We don't know yet. You'd better get dressed. We'll have to go over there straight away.'

CHAPTER TEN

ALAIN met them at his office and accompanied them to the scene of the explosion. If he was surprised at their arriving together, or at the fact that Alison was wearing her clothes from the night before, he betrayed no sign of it, either assuming that Max had called for her en route to the office and in her hurry she had simply pulled on the first clothes to hand, or mentally speculating but tactfully pretending not to notice.

Alison knew from the direction they were heading that the wrecked tent must be one of those she had cleaned out yesterday. She started to pray. Please God, let it be the empty tent that had caught fire. She breathed a sign of relief as they rounded the corner and she saw that it was. Thank God! At least no one had been hurt.

A small group of campers were already clustered around it, whispering and pointing and greeting each new development with undisguised curiosity. Quickly Max established what had happened. It seemed that the people in the next tent had smelled burning at about four a.m. They had got up, checked their own appliances and, finding them all in order, had then gone outside to try to locate the source of the acrid smell. In the darkness, flames could clearly be seen licking the inside of the neighbouring tent and, just as they had approached to see if they could extinguish the fire, there had been a small explosion, presumably the gas bottle going up. Since there was no car parked outside and no sign of movement, they had assumed the tent was unoccupied and wisely left well alone, simply despatching someone to notify the site manager at his house on site.

Now, apart from a few smouldering bits of canvas and unrecognisable lumps of molten plastic, there was little to see. Alison was about to enter the remaining skeleton of the aluminium frame to try to ascertain what had caused the fire when Max's hand on her arm detained her. 'No, wait,' he instructed. 'That is a job for the *gendarmerie* and the *Service de Protection contre l'Incendie.* We'll let them take a look first and see what they can discover.' His expression was grim.

It took a few seconds for the full import of what he was saying to reach her. The fire might not simply have been accidental, caused by some faulty piece of equipment. It could have been started deliberately . . . by the same person who had been responsible for all the other damage and thefts? But this was different. The consequences of this action could have been fatal. Did that person know that the tent would remain unoccupied, or had they simply not cared? It was almost too awful to contemplate. Mutely Alison nodded, now fully recognising the seriousness of the implications.

Some four hours later Alison was summoned to see the *Commissaire de Police,* the French equivalent of a police inspector, who had by now received the fire officer's preliminary report.

'Ah, bonjour, Mademoiselle Taylor,' he addressed her
in French as she entered the office, at the same time
indicating that she should sit down.

'Bonjour,' Alison responded with a small smile.

But the *Commissaire* did not smile back. Small in
stature and diminutive in frame, he nevertheless held
himself erect with a military-style bearing. His cold
blue eyes watched her out of an austere face whose
only concession to individuality was a neat, trim
moustache. Agatha Christie's jovial French detective,
Hercule Poirot, he most definitely was not. Alison felt
herself shiver inwardly, though she knew she had no
reason to be afraid. All he wanted was to ask her a few
questions.

'I understand that you, as one of the couriers
responsible for the Summer Canvas tents, cleaned and
re-equipped the tent concerned yesterday. Is that
correct?'

Alison nodded. 'That's right. I did it yesterday
afternoon, along with five others.'

'And you dealt with all the tents in exactly the same
way?'

'Of course, we have a standard procedure to follow.'

The *Commissaire* got up and started to pace up and
down the room. Alison wasn't quite sure why she
found the action disconcerting, but she began to feel
like a fly imprisoned in a web, watching the spider
circling. 'And did you return to the tent at all during
the evening or in the night?'

Alison shook her head. 'No, there was no need to.'

'Did you know that the expected visitors would not
be arriving last night?'

Why were his questions jumping about like this? She couldn't see any sense in them. 'Yes; when they weren't at the barbecue I went to check at the gatehouse to see if they'd arrived. There was a note on the noticeboard to say they'd phoned and that their car had broken down at the ferry port and they wouldn't be arriving until today or even Monday.'

The policeman's lips curled into a thin smile. 'Very fortunate for them, wouldn't you say, their car breaking down when it did?'

'Of course, but what . . .?'

'A moment, please, Miss Taylor, I am getting to my point. Do you have any idea what may have caused the fire?'

Alison shook her head. 'No, I was hoping you could tell me. If any of the equipment is faulty then we'll have to make a complete check of all the other tents.'

'None of the equipment was faulty.' The words fell like hard, cold snowballs.

'What . . . what caused the fire, then?' Were Max's suspicions about to prove founded?

'According to the fire officer, it was started deliberately. It seems that during the evening someone switched on the gas bottle and left a piece of wood soaked in methylated spirits smouldering in a corner of the tent. It took some time for the gas to build up, but when it reached the flames . . . boom . . . an explosion. Crude, but very effective.' He paused, as if allowing the significance of his words to sink in. Then, 'You do realise that this is not the first unexplained incident to have occurred at this site this season, Miss Taylor? However, it is the most serious.

At best, the action was designed to panic other campers. At worst, it could have been fatal.' He stressed the last word through suppressed lips.

Alison nodded and said quietly, 'I think we all realise how serious the consequences could have been.'

The police officer regarded her gravely. 'It is imperative that the person responsible be found as soon as possible.'

'Of course,' she murmured, bewildered. His glare made her feel uncomfortable. What was he trying to say? That she was in some way implicated in all of this? She was as anxious as anyone to find the culprit. She didn't think she'd find herself accused of *being* the culprit.

'I hope you will be willing to co-operate in any way possible, Miss Taylor.' The *Commissaire's* voice changed. From being low and insinuating, it became brisk and efficient. Dismissive.

'Naturally.' What else did he expect her to say? Of course she would co-operate if there was anything she could do to help.

'Good day, Miss Taylor.'

That her presence was no longer required was obvious. Not so obvious were the conclusions the policeman had drawn from their interview. His tight, veiled features gave nothing away, and Alison wasn't sure whether she had been vindicated or had incriminated herself further in his eyes.

In the evening Alison met Max for a meal in the restaurant. If anything, he had less enthusiasm for the food in front of them than she did, and when

the waitress came to remove their plates they held
little less than they had when she set them down.
Max's conversation had been desultory, to say the
least, and every effort Alison made at dialogue
seemed to fizzle into nothingness. Eventually she
abandoned all attempts and said nothing, feeling the
silence between them grow more oppressive with
every second which passed. What was the matter?
Why was Max so introspective? He seemed miles
away. She knew he must be worried about the fire,
but every effort she'd made to try to talk about it had
met with a subtle but effective rebuff.

As Alison looked at the taciturn features of the man
sitting opposite her, it was hard to believe that he was
the same passionate lover as the previous night.
Where there had been warmth and tenderness, there
was now remoteness, and she had no idea how to
transform one into the other, or if indeed it was even
in her power to transform it. Had their relationship
had the fleeting life of an exotic butterfly, emerging
from its chrysalis only to wither and die twenty-four
hours later? But, as her eyes scanned the rugged
features of the man she loved, she knew she couldn't
. . . wouldn't let it be true.

'Max, please tell me, what's the matter?' This
barrier between them had to be broken.

'You spoke to the police inspector this morning.'

Was he ignoring her question and putting one of
his own, or was he indirectly answering her? What
had the *Commissaire* said to him?

'Yes.' It was a tersely delivered monosyllable.

His eyes had a steely resolve. 'Then you realise this
problem . . . the person responsible for what

happened must be caught as soon as possible. It's imperative.'

'Of course.' Why did people keep stating the obvious to her . . . the police officer this morning and now Max?

For a moment a dark shadow flitted across his face. 'Alison . . . what I'm about to ask you . . .'

But Alison never found out what he was about to ask her. At that moment Alain's heavy frame stopped by the table. He gave Alison a quick, tight smile through pinched features, but it was Max he'd come to see. 'A new development. Can you come and have a word with Claude?' Claude was one of the regular site workers.

Max nodded, his glance flicking from Alain and back to Alison. 'I'll have to go. You understand.' Then, as he stood up from the table, 'Alison, be careful.'

Mechanically Alison nodded in turn, and it wasn't until Max and Alain had gone that she knew she should be shaking her head. It was a lie. She didn't understand. Not at all. What had he been about to ask her? Why was he telling her to be careful? Her mind could only produce one possible answer. Max had spoken to the police officer and somehow believed that she could be the culprit. The one responsible for all the damage . . . the fire. It seemed impossible, and yet what other explanation could there be for his reserve, his preoccupation, and, finally, his warning? For that was what it had been—a warning.

A cold hand worked its way round her heart, gripping it with relentless fingers, and on legs that

scarcely seemed able to support her she made her
way out of the restaurant.

Alison couldn't pinpoint the moment the idea first
occurred to her, but, once planted, the seed grew
rapidly in her mind. She wasn't the culprit and she
knew it, but maybe the only way to prove that to Max
was to expose the true culprit. On average there'd
been at least three or four incidents reported each
week since the beginning of the season, usually
occurring over a couple of nights. All had been quiet
since the fire, but surely he or she wouldn't want to
lose impetus? Weren't they likely to act again before
the end of the week? It was now Wednesday. That
only left three more nights to strike. If she kept
watch, surely she could catch them out? But first she
had to decide *whom* to watch.

It wasn't a difficult choice to make. One name
immediately sprang to mind. David. Of all the
couriers at the site, he seemed the least suited to the
work—offhand, unapproachable, inflexible. But,
more than that, there was a sly, underhand aspect to
his character which they had all noticed at times. She
perhaps more than the others. Now Alison recalled
their conversation last Saturday and his interest in
the tents she had just cleaned. Perhaps he'd had
some other plan in mind and, when he'd discovered
the tent empty, had decided on a more dramatic
project. She couldn't believe even David had actually
intended to kill anybody, but as a scare-tactic the fire
had worked wonderfully. Four families had left the
site the next day as a direct consequence of it.

Eventually Alison had worked out a plan. She

didn't mention anything to Jane, because she knew Jane would advocate going to Alain with her suspicions and letting him take action. But this was something Alison had to do herself. She had to prove to Max that she was innocent. She couldn't risk it being dismissed by Alain as feminine woolly thinking, because after all she had no proof that she was right, only her instincts.

That night she went to bed at the same time as usual but stayed awake, listening to Jane tossing and turning for what seemed an eternity. Eventually, though, faint snores could be heard coming from the neighbouring sleeping compartment and, when Alison was sure her companion was asleep, she risked movement.

She hadn't undressed, so she simply slid out of her sleeping-bag, trainers and all, and edged over to the entrance of the sleeping compartment and then across the main living area to the doorway. Every few feet she paused, but Jane's breathing remained quiet and even. The door-flap was the trickiest bit, and she edged the zip up slowly, trying to be as quiet as possible. Once outside, she decided against doing the zip up again. It was too risky. It was a warm night, so Jane wouldn't be cold. Then she crept away from the couriers' tents to a hollow between two trees some distance away, but which provided a good view, and waited.

The hands of her watch crept past midnight, then one o'clock. Perhaps David wasn't going to make any move tonight. She'd give it a bit longer. To keep herself awake Alison repeated multiplication tables in her head, then started to find names for all the letters in the alphabet. Her eyes drooped and she yawned. Good grief! If nothing happened tonight, how on earth would she keep watch like this for the next two? Her watch said two o'clock. Two hours she'd been waiting. If David was going to act tonight, surely he would have made a move by now?

Just then a shadow moved by the couriers' tents and detached itself from among them. David! It had to be. It moved quietly, watchfully, like a panther. She'd have to be careful or he would spot her. Silently she huddled her body even more tightly into the hollow of the trees, thankful that she'd had the sense to wear dark colours. His eyes peered in her direction but didn't pause, and Alison heaved a sigh of relief. Then he was heading through the bushes, bypassing the main complex, to head towards the east of the site.

Alison followed at what she hoped was a safe distance, dodging behind bushes every time the figure in front of her paused. He seemed to be heading for a section of the site where his own company's tents were situated; perhaps he reasoned that some mishap occurring there would deflect suspicion. As he neared the tents he slowed down, looked round carefully and then Alison saw him draw a huge knife out of his coat and creep towards one of the cars, obviously intending to slash the tyres. Now was the moment to act. Alison hadn't fully reasoned what she would do at this point. She'd had some idea of confronting David and had envisaged him being so shocked by her appearance that he would simply submit to her 'arrest' without a struggle. That had been her plan. It had sounded quite feasible back in the tent, but it didn't sound quite so convincing now. Nevertheless, she had to do something. If she didn't act quickly, he would simply do the damage and be gone before she could apprehend him.

She crept as close as she possibly could to him without actually coming into view, and then boldly stood up so he could see her. 'Who's that?' he hissed into the darkness.

'It's me. Alison.' She hoped her voice sounded steadier than she felt. 'I know what you're up to, David.' She continued to walk towards him. 'You've been caught.'

'It's only your word against mine,' he sneered derisively.

'You're the one who's holding the knife,' she pointed out, sounding calmer than she would ever have thought possible.

'And who's going to confirm that?' David taunted. 'I don't see any witnesses.' He took a step towards her.

For the first time Alison felt real fear. She'd assumed that once David knew he'd been rumbled he'd simply crumple like newspaper. It had never occurred to her that he would actually threaten her.

'I'm not alone,' she blurted out, knowing it to be a patent lie, but desperate now to halt David's advance and give herself time to think.

David looked round suspiciously and then leered back at her. 'Oh, I think you're pretty well alone in all of this. Even the Comte no longer seems as captivated by your charms as he was last Saturday, does he? Mind you, I suppose once he'd got what he wanted your appeal dimmed.' Snakelike, David

struck where he knew he could hurt most, at her
weakest spot, putting into words the very possibility
she been too afraid to even consider.

But if he'd thought the cruel venom would thwart
her, he was mistaken. Alison felt a bubble of rage rise
up inside her. It wasn't true. It couldn't be true. How
dared he? And the next moment she was rushing
towards him, screaming now for all she was worth.
Someone would hear, someone would come and
help her. Then she was wrestling with him,
possessed with unexpected strength as he struggled
to free himself from her grasp. She could hear
footsteps in the distance, getting nearer and nearer. If
she could only hang on for just a few more seconds.

All of a sudden there was a explosion of pain at the
side of her head. She tried to retain a hold on reality,
but the world was spinning round and round into the
distance and she was falling . . . falling into
blackness.

'She'll need to be kept quiet for a day or two, but I
don't think there's any serious damage.'

'Are you sure she doesn't need to go to hospital?'

'Quite sure. There's no sign of any fracture, but she
may have a touch of concussion. That was quite a
blow he gave her.'

Alison heard the voices as though from a long way
off. Who were they talking about? She shifted
tentatively. What had happened to the ground? She
remembered its unrelenting thud as she hit it.
Whatever she was lying on now felt infinitely soft
and accommodating in contrast.

Then the sound of a door closing quietly. With

difficulty she opened an eye to soft grey walls and heavy maroon curtains. She recognised those colours. Max's bedroom! What was she doing here? Abruptly she tried to sit upright and then winced as the dull thudding in her head protested loudly.

'Alison . . . don't.' Max's voice! The instruction came tersely from the other side of the bed, and then more gently, 'Lie down. Don't try to sit up for a while.'

Obediently Alison lay back on the pillow and turned her head towards Max. He looked grim and angry. She closed her eyes again quickly.

When she opened them again, Max hadn't disappeared as she'd rather hoped he might have, but he did look a little less stern. 'What happened?' she asked tentatively.

'Don't you remember?'

Alison shook her head slightly. She remembered everything quite clearly until the moment when David had jeered at her about Max. That had hurt. She couldn't remember anything after that.

'You tackled David, you bloody fool,' Max growled. 'You could have been killed.' His voice sounded uncharacteristically ragged.

'Oh, I don't . . .' Alison started to protest. David might be a nasty piece of work, but he wasn't a murderer.

'Dammit, don't argue, Alison. You were damn lucky it was his fist he hit you with and not the knife. Why the hell did you do it?' Max demanded roughly.

Looking at the aggrieved expression on Max's face, Alison wasn't sure why she had done it. 'I just wanted to prove to you that I hadn't caused the fire

. . . or the other incidents,' she mumbled numbly.

'What the hell are you talking about? Prove what, in God's name?' Max's voice reached a crescendo of exasperation.

'You thought I'd caused the fire, didn't you?' Alison felt like crying. Why was he being so horrible to her?

Then he was holding her hand, squeezing it so tightly that she thought he might crush it. 'Of course I didn't, you silly girl. I knew you weren't responsible.'

'But after the fire . . . you wouldn't talk to me . . . you seemed so cold . . . I thought you thought I'd caused it.'

Max raked his fingers impatiently through his hair. The way it was standing on end, it looked as if he'd done that a great many times during the night. 'And you said *I* had a habit of adding two and two and getting five,' he muttered drily.

Alison frowned. 'But . . . but you warned me to be careful.'

For a moment Max's expression softened. 'Why do women have such devious minds? Only a female could interpret being told to be careful as a warning. I told you to be careful because I didn't want anything like this to happen. Pity you didn't take some damn notice!' And the aggrieved expression was back again.

Alison wasn't at all sure she knew what he was talking about. Her brain felt woolly and nothing Max said made sense. 'But the police inspector . . . I thought he suspected me . . . I thought he must have said something to you.'

Max sighed. 'The police inspector didn't suspect you. He thought you'd been deliberately set up.'

'Me . . . set up . . . why?' Had the blow to her head damaged her brain? She wasn't following this at all.

Max took a deep breath, his voice deliberately low and controlled. 'We'd had our eye on David for some time, but he'd always been just too clever for us. He kept switching his attacks to try to cover his trail. We never knew where he'd strike next. But this last episode—that was more serious. He knew he had to put the blame more squarely on to someone else. *You*. The fact that you'd cleaned the tent out that afternoon made you the immediate suspect. He obviously didn't realise that we were already suspicious of him.'

The pattern was beginning to make more sense. 'But why did you tell *me* to be careful? Why couldn't you just arrest David?'

'We had no proof, only suspicions. That's why I was desperate to bring matters to a head. I knew David would probably strike again soon, and God knows what his warped mind might have tried to pin on you next. *That's* why I told you to be careful. And what do you do? Completely disregard my instructions and go into the attack like a one-woman army. Fortunately we'd got a man keeping watch day and night and, as soon as David made a move, he came to get Alain and myself. If we hadn't arrived when we did . . . God knows what could have happened.' Max shuddered and his hand gripped hers so tightly that Alison wondered briefly if the circulation would stop.

'What will happen to him?'

'David? I don't know. He's at the *Commissariat* now. He'll face charges for the damage he caused, but it's the people who employed him that we've also got to get.'

'Will you be able to?'

For the first time Max smiled faintly. 'I think David will squeal rather loudly under pressure. There's no honour among thieves, remember?'

So it had all worked out all right, after all. Why didn't the news bring any great satisfaction? 'At least you know Belreynac's reputation will be safe from now on.' Feebly Alison attempted to sound suitably glad, and knew she failed miserably.

'Belreynac be damned. What happened to the site was unimportant. It was *you* I was worried about.' Max's voice was a husky growl.

Was it good for her heart to start beating so wildly? Her head was swimming, and she no longer knew if it was the blow which caused the sensation or the way Max was looking at her. 'I'm all right, really I am.' It was difficult to sound like a demure convalescent when Max's face was only inches away from hers.

'But I'm not all right, Alison. When I saw David punch you tonight, I wanted to kill him. When you fell down, I wanted to breathe my own energy into you. I wanted to shake you for endangering your life in that way, and at the same time to kiss you back to consciousness. For the first time I understood what a terrible and wonderful thing it is to love someone.'

'What . . . what did you say?'

Max's face softened, lips curving in a teasing smile. 'Did you not hear me properly?'

'Max, please.' Alison didn't want to be teased right now. If Max had said what she thought he'd said, she wanted him to repeat it over and over again.

'I love you. More than I ever thought it possible to love anybody.'

Three simple words, and yet they miraculously soothed her aching limbs and throbbing head so that all Alison was aware of was the wild thumping of her heartbeat and the warmth of her own love as it pulsed through her veins. 'Oh, Max, I love you too. Very, very much.'

'How much?' Max grinned like a mischievous schoolboy.

Smiling back at him, Alison spread her arms wide. 'This much.'

'Enough to marry me?' Green eyes held hers, not doubting their answer but nevertheless wanting their confirmation.

Alison nodded, eyes sparkling. 'I thought you'd never ask.'

Max gave her chin a mock tweak. 'I shall expect less impertinence from the future Comtesse Belreynac.' But he didn't really expect to get it and doubted he would like it if he did.

Then his arms were round her in an embrace which promised never, ever to let her go, and together they watched the dawn of a new day, a golden Dordogne sunrise.

HOW FAR CAN LOVE BE CHALLENGED?

REDWOOD EMPIRE *By Elizabeth Lowell*   £2.95

The best-selling author of *'Tell Me No Lies'*, creates a bitter triangle of love and hate amidst the majestic wilderness of America's Northwest empire. 19-year old Maya Charter's marriage to Hale Hawthorne is jeopardized by her lingering feelings for her former lover – his son, Will.

CHERISH THIS MOMENT *By Sandra Canfield*   £2.75

Senator Cole Damon is Washington's most eligible bachelor, but his attraction to journalist Tracy Kent is hampered by her shocking past. If their love is to survive, he must first overcome her fear of betrayal.

BEYOND COMPARE *By Risa Kirk*   £2.50

When T.V. presenters Dinah Blake and Neil Kerrigan meet to co-host a special programme, the only thing they have in common is their growing attraction for each other. Can they settle their differences, or is their conflict a recipe for disaster?

These three new titles will be out in bookshops from March 1989.

W❂RLDWIDE

Available from Boots, Martins, John Menzies, W.H. Smith, Woolworths and other paperback stockists.

Mills & Boon
WINTER
COMPETITION

How would you like a
year's supply of Mills & Boon Romances ABSOLUTELY FREE?
Well, you can win them! All you have to do is complete the word
puzzle below and send it into us by 30th June 1989.
The first five correct entries picked out of the bag after that date
will each win a year's supply of Mills & Boon Romances (Ten
books every month - **worth over £100!**) What could be easier?

```
C W A E T A N R E B I H
H R I C E R W O L G M Y
I F R O S T A O E L U Y
L N I B O R U D R I V Y
L B L E A K B W I I N F
T O G L O V E S E A R R
S O S G O L R W I E T E
T T C H F I R E L R O E
S K A T E M Y C I K S Z
I Y R R E M I P I N E E
N A F D E C E M B E R N
N C E M I S T L E T O E
```

Ivy	Radiate	December	Star	Merry
Frost	Chill	Skate	Ski	Pine
Bleak	Glow	Mistletoe	Inn	
Boot	Ice	Fire		
Robin	Hibernate	Log		
Yule	Icicle	Scarf		
Freeze	Gloves	Berry		

**PLEASE TURN
OVER FOR
DETAILS
ON HOW
TO ENTER**

How to enter

All the words listed overleaf, below the word puzzle, are hidden in the grid. You can find them by reading the letters forwards, backwards, up or down, or diagonally. When you find a word, circle it, or put a line through it. After you have found all the words the remaining letters (which you can read from left to right, from the top of the puzzle through to the bottom) will spell a secret message.

Don't forget to fill in your name and address in the space provided and pop this page in an envelope (you don't need a stamp) and post it today. Hurry - competition ends 30th June 1989

Only one entry per household please.

Mills & Boon Competition,
FREEPOST,
P.O. Box 236,
Croydon,
Surrey CR9 9EL.

Secret message _____

_____

Name_____

Address_____

_____

_____

_____ Postcode_____